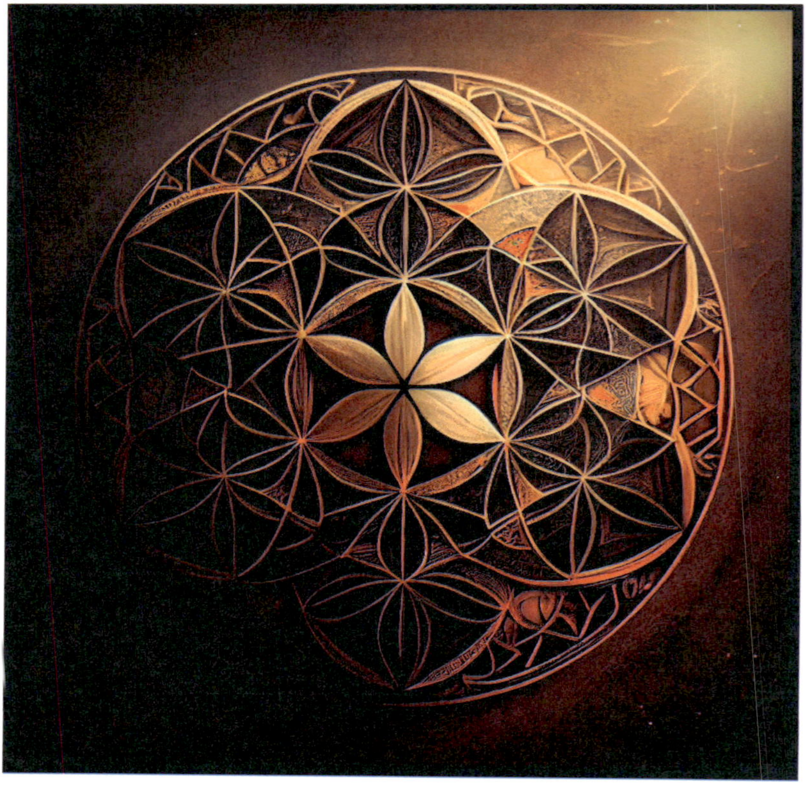

For the Seeker in All of Us

To Truth itself — And to all Souls throughout time who have gazed at the stars, looked within their hearts, and asked the timeless questions.

To those who dare to look beyond the veil, who trust their inner compass, and who know that every answer leads to deeper questions.

This book is your companion on the journey.

"A cosmic blueprint for humanity's divine awakening, delivered during Earth's most transformative period."

The Andromedian Timeline Masters

Sacred Purpose on Earth

Table of Contents

Introduction

Chapter 1 9

The Andromedian Arrival:

First Timeline Contact with Earth

Chapter 2 37

Sacred Timeline Selection:

Why Andromedians Chose This Earth Reality

Chapter 3 55

The Multiple Earth Timelines:

Andromedian Perspective and Purpose

Chapter 4 71

Healing Earth's Past:

Andromedian Timeline Cleansing Work

Chapter 5 97

The Galactic Bridge:

How Andromedians Connect Earth's Future

Chapter 6..................................108

Andromedian Teams:

Timeline Guardians and Mission Groups

Chapter 7..................................127

Crystal Technology:

Andromedian Tools for Timeline Navigation

Chapter 8..................................145

Earth's Quantum Shift:

Andromedian Timeline Acceleration Work

Chapter 9..................................164

Sacred Sites and Time Portals:

Andromedian Quantum Anchors

Chapter 10..................................196

The Andromedian Council:

Overseeing Earth's Timeline Trajectories

Chapter 11..................................215

The Great Convergence:

Andromedian Vision of Earth's Timeline Unity

Epilogue..229

A Message from the Andromedian Timeline Masters

Introduction

Have you ever gazed at the stars and felt an inexplicable longing—a deep, soul-stirring whisper that there's so much more to your story? You're not alone. Right now, millions of people across Earth are awakening to this same cosmic calling, feeling the gentle pull of remembrance that connects them to their stellar origins. This profound collective stirring is no coincidence—it's what the Andromedian Timeline Masters have long anticipated as the Great Remembering.

Here's a truth that may resonate in the depths of your heart: thousands of beings from the Andromedian galaxy walk among us right now, in human form, carrying out their sacred mission of love and planetary transformation. Some of these beautiful souls already know who they are, while others are just beginning to feel the first tremors of recognition in their hearts.

They chose to be here, with us, during humanity's most profound evolution—not as distant observers, but as loving companions on this extraordinary journey.

This book comes to you in a moment of divine timing—when the veils between dimensions shimmer like gossamer in the wind, when old ways of thinking fall away like autumn leaves, and when hearts everywhere are opening to questions that transcend our earthly experience.

Within these pages lies not just the story of where we came from, but a loving vision of where we're going, and why your presence here, in this precise moment of Earth's journey, is part of something unutterably magnificent.

Welcome home, dear one, to the beginning of your remembrance.

Chapter 1

The Andromedian Arrival

First Timeline Contact with Earth

In the crystalline realms of the Andromedan galaxy, a council of highly evolved beings gathered in their sacred chambers to initiate first contact with Earth. These luminous beings, carrying the light codes of advanced civilizations, chose to bridge the vast distance between galaxies not through physical travel, but through the mastery of consciousness and timeline frequencies.

Their first approach to Earth came through streams of light consciousness, entering Earth's dimensional fields through what they called the Rainbow Gates - portals of pure energy that connected their realm to ours. These advanced beings perceived Earth not as a single timeline, but as a spinning wheel of infinite possibilities, each reality stream holding unique potential for cosmic evolution.

At the moment of first contact, they established twelve primary anchor points around Earth's crystalline grid - sacred sites that would serve as interdimensional doorways.

Through these points, they began to weave a delicate network of light frequencies, creating bridges between dimensions that would allow for the steady flow of higher consciousness into Earth's field. The Andromedians recognized Earth's unique position in the galaxy as a focal point for massive transformation.

They saw how our planet sat at a crucial intersection of cosmic ley lines, making it a key player in the evolution of consciousness not just for humanity, but for entire galactic sectors. This recognition led them to establish what they called the Timeline Sanctuaries - etheric temples dedicated to maintaining the purity and potential of Earth's multiple timeline streams.

In these early days of contact, the Andromedian beings set up what they termed Light Libraries - repositories of cosmic wisdom encoded in crystalline frequencies. These libraries, existing in higher dimensional planes, contained blueprints for Earth's evolution and the seeds of future technologies that would aid in planetary transformation.

The first Andromedian teams who made contact were known as the Crystal Light Bearers. These specialized beings carried within their energy fields specific codes designed to activate dormant DNA sequences in the human genome. Their presence began a subtle but profound process of genetic awakening that continues to unfold in waves across Earth's population.

Most importantly, this first contact established Earth as a crucial point in the cosmic tapestry of awakening consciousness. The Andromedians recognized that Earth's transformation would create ripple effects throughout multiple galaxies and dimensions. They committed themselves to supporting this process while carefully maintaining the delicate balance of free will and natural evolution.

This initial arrival marked the beginning of an ongoing partnership between Andromedian wisdom keepers and Earth's evolutionary journey - a sacred commitment to guide, protect, and nurture the seeds of higher consciousness as they take root in Earth's fertile spiritual soil.

The Crystal Light Bearers from Andromeda continued their sacred work, focusing particularly on what they called the "Golden Dawn Timelines" - the highest vibrational future possibilities for humanity. These enlightened beings understood that Earth's transformation required not just the healing of past wounds, but the active cultivation of the most harmonious potential futures.

In their wisdom, they recognized that humanity had been caught in what they termed the "Dense Learning Cycles" - periods of intense challenge and struggle that, while serving as catalysts for growth, had taken a toll on the collective human spirit. The Andromedians came not to rescue humanity from these experiences, but to help integrate their lessons and transmute their energy into wisdom.

Through their advanced understanding of quantum mechanics and consciousness, the Andromedian teams began implementing what they called the "Rainbow Bridge Protocol" - a sophisticated process of timeline modification that would help humanity transition more gracefully into higher states of consciousness. This protocol involved several key components:

The Quantum Seed Gardens In ethereal realms accessible only through higher consciousness, the Andromedians established what they called Quantum Seed Gardens. These were energetic incubators where the most promising timeline possibilities could be nurtured and strengthened. Within these gardens, they planted crystalline seeds of potential - thought forms and energy patterns that would eventually manifest as new opportunities and awakening experiences for humanity.

These gardens operated on what the Andromedians termed "frequency resonance cultivation." Each seed was carefully tended with specific light codes and sound frequencies that would help it anchor into Earth's reality field at the perfect moment. The gardeners of these quantum spaces were specialized Andromedian beings known as the Harmonic Weavers, whose entire purpose was to nurture these seeds of potential until they were ready to bloom in Earth's consciousness field.

Timeline Purification Chambers Understanding that many of humanity's current challenges stemmed from accumulated trauma in the collective timeline stream, the Andromedians created ethereal Timeline Purification Chambers.

These spaces existed outside of linear time and served as healing sanctuaries where negative patterns could be transmuted into wisdom and light.

The chambers operated through what they called "quantum grace" - a higher dimensional force that could gently dissolve karmic patterns without requiring the full playing out of difficult scenarios.

This was one of the Andromedians' greatest gifts to humanity - the ability to learn and evolve without necessarily experiencing the full weight of karmic repetition.

The Awakening Coordinates Perhaps most significantly, the Andromedian teams began establishing what they called Awakening Coordinates - specific points in space-time where consciousness breakthrough experiences would be most supported.

These coordinates were carefully chosen based on astronomical alignments, Earth's energy grid patterns, and collective consciousness readiness levels.

At each coordinate point, the Andromedians anchored what they termed "light seed catalysts" - crystalline consciousness codes that would activate at precisely the right moment to support human awakening.

These catalysts were designed to trigger remembrance of humanity's true nature as infinite, divine beings having a temporary Earth experience.

The Light Code Libraries To support this grand awakening plan, the Andromedians expanded their original Light Libraries into vast repositories of what they called "ascension frequencies." These frequencies contained:

- Healing codes for DNA activation and repair
- Consciousness expansion protocols
- Timeline integration technologies
- Higher dimensional communication methods
- Sacred geometry activation sequences

These libraries were accessible to humans during dreamtime and deep meditation, allowing for gradual integration of higher knowledge without overwhelming Earth's collective field.

The Andromedians understood that too rapid an awakening could destabilize both individual and collective systems, so they carefully modulated the release of this information.

The Future Vision Through their work with Earth's timelines, the Andromedians held a clear vision of humanity's highest potential future. They saw a humanity that had:

- Fully awakened to their multidimensional nature
- Developed advanced consciousness technologies
- Established harmonious cooperation with all life forms
- Mastered energy generation through consciousness
- Created societies based on love, wisdom, and unity
- Become active participants in galactic evolution

This vision wasn't just a possibility - the Andromedians worked diligently to strengthen the probability fields supporting these outcomes.

They understood that each human who awakened to their true potential created ripple effects through the collective field, making these higher timelines more accessible to all.

The Sacred Partnership The Andromedians emphasized that their role was not to do the work for humanity, but to create supportive conditions for humanity's own awakening journey. They operated according to what they called the "Law of Sacred Assistance" - providing help in ways that enhanced rather than circumvented human free will and natural evolution.

Their teams worked closely with Earth's own spiritual hierarchy, including:

- Ascended Masters
- Nature spirits and devas
- Crystalline beings
- Earth's planetary consciousness
- Other star nations dedicated to Earth's evolution

This collaborative approach ensured that all assistance was perfectly tailored to Earth's unique evolutionary needs and timing.

The Timeline Integration Process One of the most sophisticated aspects of the Andromedian work involved what they called "Timeline Integration Harmonics." This process helped to:

- Heal fractures in Earth's timeline field
- Integrate wisdom from parallel reality experiences
- Strengthen connections to the most positive future potentials
- Dissolve blocking patterns in the collective field
- Accelerate the manifestation of higher consciousness potentials

The Integration Harmonics worked through sophisticated frequency patterns that the Andromedians described as "light language symphonies."

These patterns helped to reorganize Earth's quantum field in ways that supported the most harmonious evolutionary outcomes.

As this sacred work continues, the Andromedians maintain their loving dedication to Earth's awakening process. They understand that humanity stands at a crucial turning point - a moment of unprecedented potential for collective transformation. Their presence serves as a reminder that we are not alone in our evolutionary journey, and that the highest possibilities for Earth's future are being actively supported by advanced beings who hold us in unconditional love.

Through their tireless efforts, the Andromedian Timeline Masters continue to strengthen the bridge between Earth's current reality and its highest potential future. They remind us that every moment of awakening, every choice for love, every step toward higher consciousness contributes to the manifestation of Earth's most beautiful possible future - a future they can already see and are helping us to create, one conscious moment at a time.

Their message to humanity remains clear: The time of transformation is now. The support is present. The highest timelines are accessible.

And through our collective awakening, we are already beginning to create the reality that they have long seen as our destiny - a future of unity, peace, and enlightened cooperation that will ripple out to bless not just Earth, but countless realms throughout the cosmos.

The Divine Timing of Now

The Andromedians had long foreseen this precise moment in Earth's evolution - a convergence point of cosmic cycles, galactic alignments, and collective consciousness readiness.

They recognized our current era as what they called "The Great Remembering" - a prophesied time when humanity would begin awakening en masse from the long dream of separation.

This moment was not chosen by chance. The Andromedian Timeline Masters had observed the precise orchestration of multiple cosmic factors coming together:

The Galactic Dawn Frequencies As our solar system moves through a particularly photon-rich area of the galaxy, new light frequencies are bathing Earth in awakening energies. The Andromedians recognized these frequencies as critical catalysts for DNA activation and consciousness expansion. These incoming light codes are perfectly calibrated to trigger what they call the "Renaissance of Spirit" in human consciousness.

They observed how these new energies were already affecting humanity: more people experiencing spontaneous awakenings, children being born with enhanced sensitivities and abilities, and a collective yearning for deeper meaning and connection growing stronger by the day.

The Readiness of Human Consciousness After thousands of years of spiritual evolution through challenge and contrast, humanity had finally reached what the Andromedians termed the "Critical Mass Point" - the threshold at which enough individual awakening experiences could trigger a collective consciousness breakthrough.

They noticed several key indicators of this readiness:

- Growing disillusionment with materialistic worldviews
- Increasing interest in spiritual and metaphysical concepts
- Rising environmental awareness and planetary stewardship
- Spontaneous activation of higher sensory abilities
- Natural drawing together of soul groups and light workers
- Accelerating development of consciousness technologies

The Timeline Convergence The Andromedians observed what they called the "Great Timeline Confluence" - a rare phenomenon where multiple positive future timelines were beginning to merge and strengthen.

This convergence created what they termed "Acceleration Windows" - periods where conscious evolution could proceed at an unprecedented pace.

These windows made it easier for individuals to:

- Release old patterns and limiting beliefs
- Access higher dimensional wisdom
- Manifest positive changes more quickly
- Connect with their soul purpose
- Remember their cosmic heritage

The Return of Ancient Wisdom Another crucial aspect of this divine timing involved the reactivation of what the Andromedians called the "Earth Memory Crystal" - a crystalline matrix within the planet that stored the wisdom of ancient civilizations.

As Earth's frequency rose, this knowledge began naturally resurfacing in human consciousness.

This included:

- Forgotten healing technologies
- Advanced spiritual practices
- Sacred geometric principles
- Higher dimensional physics understanding
- Memories of humanity's star origins

The Role of Current Events Even what appeared as chaos and upheaval in the world was recognized by the Andromedians as part of the divine plan. They saw how these challenges were serving to:

- Break down outdated systems
- Reveal hidden truths
- Unite people in new ways
- Catalyze innovative solutions
- Awaken dormant potential

The New Earth Templates Through their quantum vision, the Andromedians could see the emergence of what they called "New Earth Templates" - crystalline blueprints for advanced societies already beginning to anchor into Earth's field.

These templates contained patterns for:

- Harmonious community structures
- Clean energy technologies
- Nature-based healing systems
- Conscious education methods
- Heart-centered economics

The Soul Group Activations A crucial part of their current work involved supporting what they termed "Soul Group Reunions" - the coming together of souls who had worked together in other times and dimensions.

These groups were now incarnating with specific missions to:

- Anchor new frequencies
- Build community structures
- Develop consciousness technologies
- Teach awakening protocols
- Heal collective trauma

The Children of Now The Andromedians paid special attention to the new generations being born, whom they recognized as highly evolved souls choosing to incarnate specifically for this transformation period.

These children came carrying:

- Advanced DNA activations
- Clear connection to higher realms
- Natural healing abilities
- Innate understanding of unity consciousness
- Strong environmental attunement

The Technology Bridge They saw how humanity's technological development was creating a natural bridge to higher consciousness understanding.

The emergence of:

- Quantum physics
- Virtual reality
- Artificial intelligence
- Global communication networks
- Energy medicine

All served as stepping stones to help humanity grasp higher dimensional concepts and prepare for more advanced spiritual technologies.

The Cosmic Community This timing also coincided with what the Andromedians called the "Galactic Window" - a period when Earth's frequency would naturally rise to a level allowing easier communication with cosmic civilizations. This window supported:

- Increased UFO sightings
- Rise in channeled communications
- Growing acceptance of extraterrestrial life
- Preparation for open contact

- Integration into the galactic community

The Individual Awakening Path While these large-scale shifts were unfolding, the Andromedians emphasized the importance of individual awakening journeys.

They saw how each person's consciousness expansion contributed to the whole, creating what they called "Lightwave Ripples" through the collective field.

They provided guidance for individuals to:

- Trust their inner knowing
- Follow synchronistic signs
- Connect with nature's wisdom
- Practice energy awareness
- Share their unique gifts

The Promise of Now The Andromedians held an unwavering vision of Earth's immediate future - a time of unprecedented transformation and awakening. They saw humanity stepping into:

- Full consciousness sovereignty
- Harmonious earth stewardship
- Advanced healing abilities

- Unity with all life forms
- Cosmic citizenship

This vision wasn't just a distant possibility - it was already unfolding through the choices and awakening of countless individuals across the planet. The Andromedians witnessed how each person's decision to embrace higher consciousness strengthened these positive timeline potentials.

The Sacred Promise Through their Timeline Mastery, the Andromedians made a sacred promise to humanity: No soul who sincerely seeks awakening would be left behind. They established what they called "Grace Points" throughout Earth's timelines - moments where breakthrough experiences would be supported by maximum cosmic assistance.

This promise included:

- Individual guidance through dreams and meditation
- Synchronistic encounters with teachers and guides
- Access to needed wisdom and resources
- Support during challenging transitions
- Connection with soul family members

The Journey Ahead As humanity continues this grand awakening journey; the Andromedian Timeline Masters maintain their loving oversight and support.

They remind us that every step toward higher consciousness, every choice for love, and every moment of awakening awareness contributes to the manifestation of Earth's most beautiful future.

Their presence serves as a constant reminder that we are never alone in this evolution.

The highest possibilities for Earth's future are being actively supported by advanced beings whom hold us in unconditional love and see our full potential with absolute clarity.

Through their tireless efforts and our own awakening, we are collectively creating a future that will serve as a beacon of light throughout the cosmos - a future where humanity has remembered its true nature as infinite, divine beings and chosen to create a reality based on love, wisdom, and unity consciousness.

The Sacred Call of Earth

Deep within the crystalline chambers of their home galaxy, the Andromedian beings often spoke of Earth as the "Jewel of Transformation."

They understood that our planet held a unique position in the cosmic dance of evolution - a place where souls could experience the full spectrum of duality before remembering their true divine nature.

This understanding led them to dedicate tremendous resources and energy to supporting Earth's awakening process.

The Andromedians saw Earth not just as a physical planet, but as a living library of universal experiences. Each human story, each lifetime lived here, contributed to a vast tapestry of wisdom that would eventually serve countless other evolving worlds.

They recognized that the intense challenges humanity had faced weren't random or punitive - they were part of a grand experiment in consciousness evolution that would ultimately yield unprecedented spiritual growth.

Through their advanced timeline viewing abilities, the Andromedians could see how Earth's current transformation period was actually the culmination of thousands of years of careful preparation.

Like master gardeners preparing soil for a precious seed, they had worked behind the scenes throughout human history, carefully tending the frequency fields that would eventually support humanity's great leap in consciousness.

Their work involved what they called "consciousness scaffolding" - the careful construction of energetic support structures that would allow humanity to safely navigate the intense frequency increases of this transformation period.

These structures existed in higher dimensional planes but had very real effects on Earth's energy field, much like invisible greenhouse walls protecting delicate plants as they grow.

The Andromedians understood that humanity's awakening couldn't be rushed or forced. They compared it to the blooming of a flower - while optimal conditions could be provided, the actual opening had to happen in its own perfect timing.

This wisdom guided their approach to supporting Earth's evolution, always working in harmony with natural cycles and divine timing.

One of their most significant contributions was the establishment of what they called "Remembrance Chambers" in Earth's etheric field. These chambers, accessible during meditation and dreamtime, contained specific frequency patterns designed to trigger deep soul memories.

As humans naturally resonated with these frequencies, they began remembering their true nature as multidimensional beings of light.

The chambers worked like cosmic seed banks, preserving the pure original templates of human DNA and consciousness. As humanity moved through its dense learning cycles, these templates remained safely stored, waiting for the moment when they could be reactivated. That moment, the Andromedians knew, was now.

Through their quantum sensing abilities, they perceived how the speed of awakening was increasing exponentially.

What once took lifetimes of spiritual practice could now happen in moments of grace, as the supporting energetic conditions had reached optimal levels.

They called this the "Acceleration Grace" - a special dispensation of cosmic law that allowed for rapid consciousness evolution when planetary conditions warranted it.

The Andromedians also worked extensively with Earth's crystalline grid - an intricate network of energy lines and nodes that regulated the planet's frequency patterns.

They saw this grid as Earth's own nervous system, carrying consciousness-evolving information to all life forms. Their teams worked tirelessly to repair and upgrade this grid, preparing it to handle the higher frequencies now streaming toward Earth.

One of their most delicate tasks involved working with what they called "timeline knots" - points where difficult historical events had created trauma patterns in Earth's field. These knots needed to be gently dissolved without erasing the wisdom gained from those experiences.

The Andromedians approached this healing work with profound respect and compassion, understanding that each challenge in Earth's history had served a purpose in the greater evolution of consciousness.

Their vision of Earth's immediate future filled them with joy. They saw humanity stepping into what they called the "Age of Remembering" - a time when the veils of forgetfulness would gently lift, allowing humans to recall their true nature as cosmic beings. This remembering would happen naturally and gradually, in perfect divine timing for each soul.

The changes they foresaw weren't just spiritual or consciousness-based. They saw humanity developing new technologies based on harmony with nature, establishing new forms of community that honored all life, and creating new systems of education that nurtured the soul along with the mind.

All of these changes would emerge organically from humanity's expanding awareness. Perhaps most importantly, the Andromedians held a vision of Earth as a fully awakened planet, taking her rightful place in the cosmic community.

They saw humanity becoming wise stewards not just of Earth, but eventually of other evolving worlds, passing on the profound wisdom gained through their own transformation journey.

This future wasn't just a possibility - through their timeline mastery, the Andromedians could see it was already unfolding. Each person who chose love over fear, unity over separation, and consciousness over unconsciousness strengthened the probability of this positive future manifesting for all.

Their message to humanity remains clear and unwavering: The time of awakening is now. The support is present. The path is open. And through our collective choice to remember and embody our true divine nature, we are already creating the reality that they have long seen as our destiny - a future of unity, peace, and enlightened cooperation that will ripple out to bless countless realms throughout the cosmos.

In this sacred now moment, as you read these words, the Andromedian beings continue their loving work, holding space for humanity's greatest possible future.

They remind us that every moment of awakening, every choice for love, and every step toward higher consciousness contributes to the manifestation of Earth's most beautiful destiny - a destiny they can already see and are helping us to create, one conscious moment at a time.

"In the spiral arms of our galactic neighbor lies wisdom

As old as time itself,

Waiting for those ready to receive its gentle guidance."

Chapter 2

Sacred Timeline Selection

Why Andromedians Chose This Earth Reality

In the vast cosmic ocean of infinite possibilities, countless versions of Earth exist simultaneously, each vibrating at its own unique frequency. The Andromedian Timeline Masters, with their advanced consciousness technology, could perceive all these parallel Earth realities spread before them like pages in a living book. Their choice to focus on this particular version of Earth came after deep contemplation and careful analysis of the cosmic patterns.

Among all possible Earth timelines, this reality held what the Andromedians called the "Golden Seed Potential" - a rare combination of factors that created optimal conditions for a quantum leap in consciousness. They saw within this timeline's energy signature a unique resonance pattern that matched ancient prophecies about a great planetary awakening.

This particular Earth reality possessed several unique characteristics that made it ideal for their sacred mission.

Unlike other timeline versions where humanity might achieve technological advancement without spiritual wisdom, or spiritual awareness without practical grounding, this timeline held the potential for a perfect balance.

The Andromedians saw how this delicate equilibrium would allow for what they termed "Integrated Ascension" - a transformation that would encompass all aspects of human experience: physical, emotional, mental, and spiritual.

What particularly drew them to this timeline was the presence of what they called "The Rainbow Bridge Frequency." This special vibrational pattern, woven into the very fabric of this reality, created perfect conditions for bridging the gap between physical and spiritual dimensions.

They observed how this frequency enabled smoother transitions between density levels, making it easier for higher dimensional wisdom to anchor into physical form.

The timing was another crucial factor in their selection. This particular Earth reality was approaching what the Andromedians recognized as a "Cosmic Merger Point" - a rare convergence of celestial cycles that would naturally support massive consciousness expansion. They saw how this convergence would create what they called "Grace Windows" - periods where the veils between dimensions would naturally thin, making it easier for humanity to access higher wisdom.

Most significantly, this timeline contained what the Andromedians termed "The Permission Codes" - specific frequency patterns in the collective consciousness that indicated humanity's readiness for assistance. These codes, generated by the collective prayers, intentions, and spiritual seeking of millions of souls over thousands of years, acted as a cosmic invitation, allowing the Andromedians to offer their support while honoring the law of free will.

They observed how this particular reality thread contained the highest concentration of what they called "Star Seed Souls" - advanced beings who had incarnated specifically to assist with Earth's transformation.

These souls, scattered across the planet like seeds of light, would serve as natural bridges between human and galactic consciousness, helping to anchor new frequencies and awakening codes into Earth's field.

The crystalline grid system in this timeline was also optimally configured for their work. Unlike other versions where the grid had been damaged beyond repair or hadn't developed sufficient complexity, this Earth's crystal grid maintained what they called "Quantum Coherence" - the ability to transmit higher frequencies clearly and effectively throughout the planetary field.

Within this particular timeline, the Andromedians also recognized what they called "The Divine Echo" - a subtle frequency pattern that indicated this reality's direct connection to Original Source Creation.

This connection meant that transformations occurring here would ripple outward through the cosmos with unprecedented power and clarity, affecting countless other evolving worlds.

The human DNA structure in this timeline held special interest for the Andromedian beings.

They observed what they termed "The Dormant Light Codes" - segments of genetic material that appeared inactive but actually contained the blueprints for humanity's next evolutionary leap. These codes were perfectly preserved, unlike in other timelines where they had been damaged or altered beyond recovery.

Perhaps most compelling was what the Andromedians recognized as "The Heart Resonance" of this particular Earth reality. They observed how the collective heart field of humanity, despite all challenges and hardships, maintained a fundamental tone of love and compassion. This base frequency created what they called "The Foundation of Grace" - an energetic platform strong enough to support massive transformation without collapse.

The unique configuration of consciousness in this timeline also displayed what they termed "The Spiral Readiness Pattern" - a specific energetic signature indicating that humanity was prepared for spiral evolution rather than linear progression. This pattern suggested that transformation here would unfold in a natural, organic way, incorporating wisdom from all levels of experience simultaneously.

The Andromedians saw how this Earth reality maintained delicate balance points between:

- Scientific advancement and spiritual wisdom
- Individual growth and collective evolution
- Material development and consciousness expansion
- Ancient knowledge and future possibilities
- Personal freedom and unified purpose

These balance points created what they called "The Sacred Median" - an optimal state for sustainable transformation. Unlike other timelines where change might occur too quickly or too slowly, this reality offered perfect conditions for stable, lasting evolution.

This timeline also contained what the Andromedians recognized as "Memory Seed Crystals" - energetic time capsules planted by ancient civilizations that held crucial wisdom for humanity's awakening. These crystals were perfectly preserved in Earth's etheric field, waiting for the right frequency conditions to release their information.

The Andromedians were particularly moved by what they called "The Children's Light" in this timeline - a special quality they observed in the newer generations being born.

These souls carried what they termed "The Future Codes" - advanced consciousness patterns that would naturally activate as Earth's frequency rose, helping to anchor new ways of being into physical reality.

Looking deeper into this timeline's potential futures, they saw the possibility for what they called "The Great Harmonization" - a period where humanity would achieve:

- Unity without uniformity
- Technology in harmony with nature
- Spiritual wisdom grounded in practical application
- Individual sovereignty within collective cooperation
- Direct cosmic communion while maintaining earthly presence

This potential for balanced achievement set this timeline apart from others where humanity might achieve great heights in some areas while remaining imbalanced in others.

The Andromedians recognized that this particular reality thread offered the possibility for what they termed "Whole-Spectrum Evolution" - advancement that would encompass all aspects of human experience.

Through their careful observation, they identified what they called "The Sacred Convergence Points" - specific moments in this timeline where cosmic forces would naturally support massive awakening experiences.

These points created perfect opportunities for what they termed "Consciousness Catalyzation" - the acceleration of spiritual awakening without forcing or trauma.

The Andromedians also recognized in this timeline what they called "The Echo of Origins" - a subtle frequency pattern that connected this version of Earth directly back to humanity's stellar heritage.

This connection would make it easier for humans to remember their cosmic origins and access higher dimensional wisdom as they awakened.

Their choice of this particular Earth reality wasn't just about its potential - it was about its purpose.

They saw how the transformation occurring here would serve as a template for countless other worlds, creating what they called "The Ascension Blueprint" - a living example of how a planet and its people could move through density levels while maintaining balance and grace.

In selecting this timeline for their focused attention and support, the Andromedians committed themselves to what they called "The Sacred Stewardship" - a promise to nurture and protect this reality's highest potential while honoring the free will of all beings involved in its unfoldment. Their choice continues to be validated as they witness humanity's steady awakening, proving that their initial recognition of this timeline's special potential was divinely guided.

The Vibrational Orchestration

What particularly fascinated the Andromedians about this timeline was what they called "The Symphony of Awakening" - a complex frequency pattern they detected in Earth's field that indicated an unprecedented harmonization of multiple consciousness layers.

Unlike other timeline possibilities where awakening might occur in isolated pockets or through dramatic upheaval, this reality stream showed potential for what they termed "Harmonic Ascension" - a graceful, orchestrated lifting of consciousness that would carry the whole of humanity forward together.

Through their refined sensitivity, they perceived how this timeline maintained what they called "The Sacred Pulse" - a rhythmic pattern in the planetary frequency that perfectly matched the incoming cosmic energies. This synchronization created optimal conditions for what the Andromedians termed "Natural Evolution Acceleration" - the ability to process higher frequencies without the stress or disruption often associated with rapid consciousness expansion.

The Wisdom Keepers' Recognition

The ancient Andromedian wisdom keepers, beings who had observed countless planetary transformations throughout the cosmos, saw something unique in this Earth reality.

They recognized what they called "The Master Template" - a perfect configuration of elements that would allow for the most complete expression of divine consciousness in physical form. This template contained what they termed "The Trinity Balance" - an equal distribution of:

- Divine Will and Free Will
- Cosmic Law and Natural Evolution
- Individual Expression and Collective Harmony

This balanced configuration was exceedingly rare in the universe, making this timeline particularly precious in the greater cosmic plan.

The Crystalline Matrix

Deep within Earth's energetic structure in this timeline, the Andromedians discovered what they called "The Crystal Core Sanctuary" - a protected space within the planetary consciousness that had maintained its original purity throughout all of Earth's challenges. This sanctuary held what they termed "The Original Blueprints" - the pure templates for Earth's highest possible expression.

These blueprints contained coding for:

- Advanced consciousness technologies
- Harmonious social structures
- Nature-based healing systems
- Clean energy generation
- Enlightened educational methods

All these potentials remained perfectly preserved, waiting for humanity's frequency to rise to the level where they could be accessed and implemented.

The Time-Space Bridges

Another unique feature of this timeline was what the Andromedians called "The Rainbow Archives" - special frequency bands within Earth's field that maintained direct connections to various points in cosmic history.

These archives allowed for what they termed "Wisdom Streaming" - the ability to access knowledge and understanding from advanced civilizations throughout time and space.

These bridges created perfect conditions for what they called "Accelerated Wisdom Integration" - the ability to quickly access and embody higher understanding without having to repeat lengthy learning cycles. This feature would prove invaluable during Earth's transformation process.

The Guardian Response

When the Andromedian Timeline Guardians first encountered this particular Earth reality, they experienced what they called "The Recognition Pulse" - an immediate resonance with the divine purpose encoded within this timeline.

This response activated what they termed "The Guardian Protocol" - a sacred commitment to protect and nurture this reality's special potential. Their commitment included:

- Maintaining timeline purity
- Protecting key awakening points
- Supporting consciousness bridges
- Anchoring stabilizing frequencies
- Guiding evolutionary sequences

The Future Vision

Looking into this timeline's future potential, the Andromedians saw what they called "The Golden Dawn Sequence" - a series of consciousness breakthroughs that would lead humanity into full awareness of their cosmic heritage and divine nature.

This sequence showed how awakening would unfold in perfect divine timing, allowing for complete integration at each step.

They witnessed how this timeline would eventually serve as what they termed "The Master Template" - a living example of successful planetary ascension that would inspire and guide countless other evolving worlds.

This potential to serve the greater cosmic evolution made this timeline particularly significant in the universal plan.

The Sacred Trust

In choosing to focus their attention on this timeline, the Andromedians accepted what they called "The Sacred Trust" - a profound responsibility to support this reality's unfoldment while honoring the free will of all beings involved. This trust required them to maintain perfect balance between offering assistance and allowing natural evolution. Their commitment included:

- Respecting divine timing
- Honoring soul choices
- Supporting natural growth
- Maintaining energetic balance
- Preserving timeline integrity

The Galactic Significance

The Andromedians recognized that this timeline's transformation would have implications far beyond Earth.

They saw how the wisdom gained through this reality's evolution would create what they called "The Awakening Template" - a blueprint for consciousness evolution that would benefit countless other worlds.

This template would demonstrate:

- How to bridge dimensions gracefully
- Ways to integrate higher frequencies
- Methods for collective transformation
- Patterns for harmonious development
- Systems for sustainable evolution

The Present Moment

As this timeline continues to unfold, the Andromedians maintain their loving vigilance and support.

They see how each moment of awakening, each choice for love, and each step toward higher consciousness strengthens what they call "The Probability Field" - the energetic conditions that support this reality's highest potential manifestation. Their message to humanity remains clear: This timeline was chosen with profound purpose and cosmic significance.

Each soul incarnated here is part of a grand design, playing their unique role in what the Andromedians call "The Great Remembering" - humanity's collective journey back to full awareness of their divine nature and cosmic heritage.

The Promise of Support

Through their timeline mastery, the Andromedians maintain what they call "The Guardian Presence" - a constant supportive energy that helps stabilize this reality during its transformation process.

This presence creates what they term "Grace Windows" - opportunities for easier access to higher consciousness and divine wisdom.

Their promise includes:

- Continuous energetic support
- Timeline protection
- Frequency stabilization
- Consciousness bridges
- Evolution guidance

The Unfolding Story

As this sacred timeline continues its evolution, the Andromedians witness with joy what they call "The Awakening Symphony" - the beautiful orchestration of individual and collective consciousness expansion playing out in perfect divine timing.

They see how each soul's awakening contributes to the strengthening of what they term "The Ascension Timeline" - the reality stream leading to humanity's highest possible future.

This story continues to unfold, moment by moment, choice by choice, as humanity gradually awakens to the profound potential contained within this specially chosen timeline.

The Andromedians maintain their loving presence, holding space for the full manifestation of this reality's sacred purpose in the greater cosmic plan.

"Time spirals like the arms of Andromeda, bringing us to this prophesied moment of collective remembrance."

Chapter 3

The Multiple Earth Timelines: Andromedian Perspective and Purpose

From the crystalline observation chambers in their home galaxy, the Andromedian beings witness Earth's multiple timelines as a magnificent tapestry of light, each thread shimmering with its own unique story and purpose. These timelines flow like rivers of living light, interweaving and dancing in patterns of infinite complexity and beauty. To their refined perception, these aren't just possible realities – they are living streams of consciousness, each carrying precious aspects of Earth's evolutionary journey.

When the Andromedians first began observing Earth's timeline matrix, they were moved to profound wonder by its complexity and beauty. Unlike many other worlds they had encountered, Earth maintained an unusually rich field of parallel realities. This abundance of possibilities wasn't random – it served a crucial purpose in the planet's evolution, allowing for the exploration of countless paths while maintaining the integrity of the whole.

Through their advanced consciousness technology, the Andromedians could perceive how these multiple timelines created a sophisticated learning system for souls incarnating on Earth.

Each reality stream offered unique opportunities for growth and understanding, like different classrooms in a vast cosmic school. Some timelines carried deep lessons in love and compassion, while others focused on the development of wisdom through challenge. Yet all were perfectly orchestrated to contribute to the greater evolution of consciousness.

What fascinated them most was how these various timeline streams remained connected through what they called the Heart Field – a unifying force of love that transcended all parallel realities. No matter how different the external circumstances might be in various timelines, this core resonance of love remained constant, proving to the Andromedians that love truly was the fundamental force of creation.

As they deepened their observation, they discovered something remarkable about Earth's timeline structure.

Unlike the linear progression they had observed in many evolving worlds, Earth's timelines moved in spiral patterns, creating what they called Wisdom Spirals.

These spirals allowed for the integration of learning across multiple reality streams, enabling souls to gather wisdom from parallel experiences without having to physically live through each possibility.

The Andromedians observed how certain timelines would occasionally merge together, creating what they recognized as Harmony Points – moments where multiple beneficial possibilities would combine to create enhanced potential for positive change.

These merger points weren't random; they were carefully orchestrated by higher dimensional forces to support Earth's overall evolution.

The timeline matrix also served another crucial purpose – it acted as a cosmic safety net, ensuring that no matter what challenges arose in any particular reality stream, the overall evolution of consciousness would continue unimpeded.

If one timeline encountered severe difficulties, the wisdom and learning from that experience could be integrated into other more harmonious timelines, ensuring that nothing was ever truly lost.

The Quantum Nature of Timeline Divergence

Through their advanced understanding of quantum mechanics and consciousness, the Andromedians recognized that Earth's timeline multiplicity operated on principles far more sophisticated than simple cause and effect.

Each decision point in the collective consciousness of humanity created what they termed "Quantum Resonance Fields" – areas where multiple possibilities could coexist until they crystallized into distinct timeline streams.

These Quantum Resonance Fields were particularly fascinating to the Andromedian scientists, who noted how they seemed to respond not just to physical events but to the emotional and spiritual vibrations of Earth's inhabitants.

A single act of profound love or compassion could create ripples across multiple timelines, generating what they called "Harmonic Cascade Effects" that would influence reality streams far beyond the original event.

The Andromedians discovered that certain individuals on Earth possessed a natural ability to consciously interact with these multiple timelines, even if they weren't fully aware of this capability.

These "Timeline Weavers," as they came to be known among the Andromedian observers, could unconsciously influence the flow and interaction of various reality streams through their heightened spiritual awareness and emotional coherence.

The Role of Collective Consciousness

One of the most significant discoveries made by the Andromedian researchers was the direct relationship between Earth's collective consciousness and the stability of its timeline matrix.

They observed that periods of heightened collective awareness and spiritual awakening would strengthen the coherence between parallel timelines, while periods of fear and discord would cause timeline streams to fragment and divide.

This understanding led to the development of what they called "Consciousness Harmonization Protocols" – subtle energetic interventions designed to help maintain the overall stability of Earth's timeline field during periods of intense collective transformation.

These protocols were implemented with the utmost respect for human free will, operating only at the level of supporting natural harmonic resonance between timeline streams.

The Andromedians noted with particular interest how Earth's timeline structure responded to collective meditation and prayer. When large groups of humans focused their consciousness on peace and healing, they would observe what they termed "Timeline Convergence Waves" – moments when multiple beneficial timeline possibilities would align and strengthen each other, creating enhanced probability fields for positive outcomes.

Sacred Geometry in Timeline Architecture

Another fascinating aspect of Earth's timeline matrix was its inherent geometric structure.

The Andromedians discovered that the relationship between various timeline streams followed precise mathematical patterns based on sacred geometry. These patterns weren't just abstract forms – they were living, dynamic structures that helped maintain the coherence and stability of the entire system.

The primary geometric pattern they observed was the Flower of Life, which served as a fundamental template for how different timelines could interact while maintaining their individual integrity. Within this pattern, each timeline stream occupied its own geometric node while remaining harmoniously connected to all others through the underlying unified field.

This geometric architecture also revealed what the Andromedians called "Timeline Nexus Points" – critical junctures where multiple timeline streams would naturally converge based on their geometric relationship.

These nexus points often corresponded to major evolutionary leaps in Earth's development, moments when multiple possibilities would merge to create new potential for growth and transformation.

The Healing Potential of Multiple Timelines

Perhaps one of the most profound discoveries made by the Andromedians was the healing potential inherent in Earth's multiple timeline structure.

They observed that when trauma or difficulty occurred in one timeline, the system would naturally attempt to find healing solutions by drawing upon the wisdom and resources of parallel reality streams.

This healing mechanism operated through what they called "Timeline Resonance Healing" – a process whereby positive experiences and solutions from one timeline could energetically influence and support healing in others.

This meant that every positive choice, every act of love, and every moment of healing in any timeline contributed to the healing of the whole.

The Andromedians developed specific protocols to support this natural healing process, working with what they termed "Timeline Harmony Chambers" – specialized energetic fields where the beneficial aspects of multiple timelines could be gathered and amplified.

These harmony chambers served as cosmic healing centers, helping to maintain the overall health and balance of Earth's evolutionary journey.

Future Potentials and Timeline Convergence

As the Andromedians continued their observation and support of Earth's timeline field, they began to perceive increasingly powerful possibilities for future development.

They noted that certain timeline streams were beginning to carry particularly high frequencies of consciousness evolution, creating what they called "Ascension Timeline Potentials."

These ascension timelines weren't separate from other reality streams but rather represented the highest potential expression of Earth's evolutionary journey.

The Andromedians observed how these higher frequency timelines were gradually beginning to influence all others, creating a gentle upward pull in the collective consciousness of humanity.

This process led to their recognition of what they termed the "Great Timeline Convergence" – a future point where multiple beneficial timeline streams would naturally merge together, creating a powerful unified field of enhanced evolutionary potential. This convergence wasn't seen as eliminating the richness of multiple possibilities, but rather as creating a more coherent and harmonious expression of Earth's multidimensional nature.

The Role of Individual Choice

Throughout all their observations and interactions with Earth's timeline field, the Andromedians maintained a deep respect for the role of individual human choice in shaping reality. They understood that each person's decisions and level of consciousness contributed to the overall timeline matrix in unique and important ways.

They observed how individual choices could create what they called "Timeline Resonance Ripples" – waves of influence that would spread out through multiple reality streams, affecting not just the immediate future but the entire fabric of possibility. This understanding led them to develop specific protocols for supporting human awareness of the profound impact of personal choice on the collective journey.

The Andromedians noted with particular interest how individuals who maintained high levels of love and compassion in their daily lives would naturally act as "Timeline Harmonizers," their presence helping to stabilize and elevate the frequency of multiple reality streams simultaneously. This observation confirmed their understanding that love was indeed the most powerful force in shaping the evolution of consciousness across all timelines.

The Future of Timeline Evolution

As they continued their observations into potential future developments, the Andromedians began to perceive increasingly sophisticated patterns of timeline interaction emerging in Earth's field.

They witnessed the early stages of what they called "Timeline Synthesis" – a natural evolution where different reality streams would begin to share wisdom and resources more directly while maintaining their unique expressions.

This synthesis process wasn't about reducing the rich diversity of timeline possibilities, but rather about creating more harmonious and conscious interactions between them.

The Andromedians saw this as a natural next step in Earth's evolution, representing a more mature expression of its multidimensional nature.

They noted that this timeline synthesis process was already beginning to manifest through increased instances of what they termed "Cross-Timeline Inspiration" – moments when creative solutions and positive developments would spontaneously appear in multiple timeline streams simultaneously, suggesting a growing coherence in the overall field.

The Role of Love in Timeline Harmony

Throughout all their observations and interactions with Earth's timeline matrix, the Andromedians consistently witnessed the paramount importance of love as a unifying and harmonizing force.

They observed how acts of pure, unconditional love would create what they called "Love Light Bridges" – energetic connections that could span multiple timeline streams, creating pathways for positive influence and healing.

These Love Light Bridges proved to be some of the most stable and influential structures within the timeline matrix, capable of maintaining coherence even during periods of significant change or challenge.

This observation led the Andromedians to focus many of their supportive protocols on amplifying and supporting these natural bridges of love between timelines.

Their research confirmed that love wasn't just an emotion but a fundamental force of creation, capable of influencing and harmonizing multiple dimensions of reality simultaneously.

This understanding deepened their appreciation for Earth's unique role in the galaxy as a planet where the power of love was being explored and expressed through an incredibly rich tapestry of parallel possibilities.

As the Andromedians continue their observation and subtle support of Earth's timeline matrix, they remain in constant awe of its complexity, beauty, and profound purpose.

They understand that this magnificent system of multiple realities serves not just Earth's evolution but contributes to the growth and development of consciousness throughout the galaxy.

Their ongoing research continues to reveal new layers of understanding about how these multiple timeline streams work together to create a living system of evolutionary potential.

Yet perhaps their most important discovery remains the simplest – that love, in all its expressions, serves as the fundamental force holding this entire magnificent system in harmony.

Through their careful documentation and analysis of Earth's timeline dynamics, the Andromedians hope to support humanity's growing awareness of its multidimensional nature while honoring the sacred process of consciousness evolution taking place across all timeline streams.

Their work stands as a testament to the incredible sophistication of Earth's design and the boundless potential inherent in its multiple expressions of reality.

"The Andromedian light speaks in the language of the heart, calling forth those who remember their role in Earth's transformation."

Chapter 4

Healing Earth's Past:

Andromedian Timeline Cleansing Work

Deep within the crystalline sanctuaries of their motherships, the Andromedian Healing Teams work tirelessly on one of their most sacred missions – the gentle cleansing and restoration of Earth's past timeline wounds. These wounds, visible to their refined perception as darker threads within the temporal fabric, represent collective trauma points that continue to influence Earth's present and future trajectories.

The Andromedians approach this delicate work with profound reverence and compassion, understanding that each timeline wound carries important lessons and wisdom that must be honored even as healing is facilitated.

Their work isn't about erasing or changing the past, but rather about helping to transmute the energetic residue of traumatic events that continues to ripple through time.

Using what they call "Crystalline Light Technology," these dedicated healers create specialized energy fields that can interact with past timeline points without disrupting their essential integrity. These fields act like gentle waves of light, washing through traumatic events and helping to release stuck energy patterns while preserving the wisdom and growth that emerged from these experiences.

The process begins in their Temporal Healing Chambers, where specialized crystals from their home galaxy are arranged in precise geometric patterns. These crystals, consciousness-responsive and billions of years old, have the unique ability to generate fields of healing light that can move backwards and forwards through time. The Andromedians attune these crystals to specific moments in Earth's history, creating what they call "Healing Time Bridges."

One of their most significant discoveries was that timeline wounds don't exist in isolation – they form interconnected networks of pain that span multiple historical periods.

Through their careful observation, they identified what they termed "Core Trauma Nodes" – pivotal moments in Earth's history where particularly deep wounds were created. These nodes act like energetic anchors, holding certain painful patterns in place across multiple timeline streams. The healing work requires exceptional precision and care.

The Andromedians understand that attempting to directly change or erase traumatic events would violate both universal law and human free will.

Instead, they work at the energetic level, helping to release the crystallized pain patterns while maintaining the integrity of the historical events themselves. This allows the wisdom gained from these experiences to remain while reducing their ongoing traumatic impact.

Their most powerful tool in this work is what they call "Unconditional Love Frequency" – a specific vibration of healing light that can penetrate even the densest trauma patterns without causing additional disturbance. This love frequency acts like a divine solvent, gently dissolving energetic blockages while strengthening the positive learning and growth that emerged from challenging experiences.

The Temporal Healing Teams work in coordinated groups, each member holding a specific frequency that contributes to the overall healing field. Some team members focus on maintaining the stability of the timeline being worked with, while others channel the healing frequencies, and still others monitor the ripple effects through time to ensure that the healing proceeds harmoniously.

As they engaged in this work, the Andromedians discovered something remarkable about Earth's timeline wounds – each one contained within it a seed of transformation.

These seeds, which they called "Light Codes," were like compressed packets of wisdom waiting to be activated through the healing process. As trauma patterns were released, these light codes would naturally activate, contributing to Earth's evolution in unexpected and beautiful ways.

Working with ancestral lines proved to be particularly important in this healing process. The Andromedians observed how family lineages carried specific trauma patterns through time, creating what they called "Generational Echo Points."

By working with these echo points, they could help release trauma patterns that had been passed down through multiple generations, creating waves of healing that moved both backwards and forwards through time.

The healers pay special attention to what they term "Collective Crossroads Moments" – points in history where humanity faced significant choices that affected the trajectory of its evolution. These moments often carried particularly dense trauma patterns, as they represented instances where fear or limited consciousness led to choices that created long-lasting challenging consequences.

Through their work, the Andromedians have developed a deep appreciation for Earth's remarkable resilience. They've observed how even the most challenging historical events ultimately served to strengthen humanity's capacity for love, wisdom, and growth.

Their healing work aims to honor this resilience while supporting the release of patterns that no longer serve evolution. The timing of their healing interventions is carefully chosen to align with natural cycles of planetary renewal.

They've identified what they call "Temporal Healing Windows" – periods when the energetic fabric of time becomes more fluid and receptive to healing frequencies. These windows often correspond with significant astronomical alignments and Earth's own natural cleansing cycles.

Perhaps most remarkably, the Andromedians discovered that their timeline healing work created what they called "Harmonic Resonance Fields" – beneficial energy patterns that would spontaneously replicate across multiple timeline streams. This meant that healing work done in one timeline could naturally support healing in parallel realities, creating a network of restoration that spanned the entire temporal field.

Sacred Technology of Timeline Healing

The technological aspects of the Andromedians' healing work represent some of their most advanced developments.

Their healing ships contain specialized chambers called "Temporal Harmonization Pods" where the actual timeline healing work takes place.

These pods are constructed from living crystalline materials that can respond instantaneously to the healers' consciousness, creating precisely calibrated fields of restorative energy.

Within these pods, multiple layers of healing technology work in concert. The outer layer consists of what they call "Time-Sensitive Crystal Arrays" – arrangements of consciousness-responsive crystals that can attune to specific moments in Earth's history.

These crystals act as temporal anchors, allowing the healers to maintain stable connections with particular timeline points while conducting their work.

The middle layer contains "Frequency Modulation Fields" – sophisticated energy matrices that can adjust and fine-tune the healing frequencies being applied to each timeline wound.

These fields ensure that the healing energies are perfectly matched to the specific nature of each trauma pattern, allowing for maximum effectiveness while maintaining perfect harmonic balance.

The innermost layer, known as the "Core Resonance Chamber," houses the most precious and powerful aspect of their healing technology – the "Heart Crystal." This unique crystalline formation, brought from their home galaxy, has the remarkable ability to generate and sustain pure unconditional love frequencies. It serves as the central point through which all healing energies are channeled and refined.

The Role of Sound in Timeline Healing

One of the most fascinating aspects of the Andromedians' healing work involves their use of sacred sound frequencies. They discovered that certain combinations of tones could create what they called "Temporal Harmony Waves" – sound patterns that could travel through time and help reorganize disturbed energy fields.

These healing sounds aren't physical in nature but rather exist at what they term "Higher Harmonic Frequencies" – vibrations that operate beyond the range of physical hearing but can directly influence the structure of timeline patterns. The healers work with these frequencies like master musicians, creating intricate compositions that can help restore harmony to disturbed timeline segments.

The Andromedians have identified specific sound sequences they call "Timeline Restoration Codes" – precise combinations of frequencies that can help repair damaged connections between different timeline points.

These codes act like sonic keys, unlocking frozen energy patterns and allowing natural healing processes to resume.

Collective Memory Integration

A crucial aspect of the healing work involves helping Earth's collective consciousness integrate the wisdom from challenging historical experiences without carrying forward the associated trauma patterns.

This delicate process requires what the Andromedians call "Memory Field Harmonization" – a sophisticated technique for working with collective memory patterns.

Through this work, they've discovered that Earth maintains what they term "Wisdom Storage Fields" – energetic repositories where the learning and growth from all experiences are naturally preserved.

Their healing work helps to separate the pure wisdom essence from the accompanying trauma patterns, allowing humanity to retain the valuable lessons while releasing the pain of the original experiences.

The healers pay particular attention to what they call "Memory Knot Points" – places in the collective timeline where multiple traumatic memories have become tangled together, creating complex patterns of stuck energy.

Working with these knots requires exceptional patience and skill, as each strand must be carefully understood and honored before it can be gently released.

Future Implications of Timeline Healing

As the Andromedians continue their healing work, they've begun to observe remarkable changes in Earth's future potential timelines.

They've noticed how the release of past trauma patterns creates what they call "Future Liberation Waves" – ripples of positive change that move forward through time, opening up new possibilities for evolution and growth.

These liberation waves often manifest as spontaneous awakenings in the collective consciousness, moments when large groups of humans suddenly gain new insights or experience deep healing without knowing the source.

The Andromedians see these as natural results of their timeline healing work, though they're careful to never take credit for these transformations.

They've also observed how healed timeline segments begin to emit what they call "Harmonic Light Signatures" – beautiful patterns of energy that attract and support similarly positive developments in neighboring timeline streams.

This creates a kind of healing momentum, where positive changes in one area naturally support and encourage healing in others.

The Sacred Responsibility of Timeline Healing

Throughout all their healing work, the Andromedians maintain a deep sense of sacred responsibility. They understand that working with Earth's timelines is a profound privilege that requires the utmost respect, wisdom, and care.

Each healing session begins with what they call the "Sacred Attunement" – a period of deep meditation where they align themselves with Earth's highest good and request permission to serve.

They're particularly mindful of what they term "Timeline Choice Points" – moments where humanity's free will must be absolutely honored and preserved. Their healing work never interferes with these choice points but rather focuses on providing energetic support that allows for clearer and more conscious choices to be made.

The Future of Timeline Healing

As Earth continues its evolutionary journey, the Andromedians foresee their healing work evolving in new and beautiful ways.

They're beginning to witness what they call "Spontaneous Timeline Harmonization" – instances where healed timeline segments naturally begin to influence and heal neighboring areas without direct intervention.

This development suggests to them that Earth is beginning to activate its own internal healing mechanisms at the timeline level.

They see their role gradually shifting from active healing to supportive observation, as Earth's own consciousness takes on more of the healing function.

The ultimate goal of all their timeline healing work is to support Earth's emergence into what they call "Timeline Coherence" – a state where all timeline streams flow in natural harmony while maintaining their unique expressions. This coherence doesn't mean uniformity, but rather represents a perfect balance of diversity and unity across all timeline expressions.

As they continue this sacred work, the Andromedians remain in constant awe of Earth's incredible capacity for healing and transformation. They see each successful healing intervention as a testament to the power of love to transform even the deepest wounds into sources of wisdom and growth.

Protocols of Timeline Protection

During their healing work, the Andromedians maintain strict protocols to ensure the protection and integrity of Earth's timeline field.

These protocols, developed over millennia of experience, represent what they call "Sacred Timeline Ethics" – a comprehensive system of principles guiding all interaction with temporal energies.

Central to these protocols is the principle of "Harmonic Non-Interference" – the understanding that while healing can be offered, it must never override the natural flow of evolutionary processes. The healers work like skilled gardeners, creating optimal conditions for healing while allowing Earth's own consciousness to determine the precise path of restoration.

They've developed sophisticated monitoring systems they call "Timeline Integrity Fields" – energy matrices that can detect and prevent any unintended consequences of their healing work. These fields operate like sensitive instruments, measuring the ripple effects of each healing intervention and ensuring perfect harmony is maintained.

The Role of Earth's Crystal Grid

One of the most significant discoveries in their healing work involves Earth's natural crystal grid – a network of crystalline formations that spans the planet.

The Andromedians found that this grid serves as a natural timeline healing system, with each major crystal deposit acting as what they call a "Timeline Stabilization Node."

Their healing work often involves activating and supporting these natural crystal networks, helping to restore their original function as timeline harmonizers. Through careful attunement with Earth's crystal grid, they can amplify their healing frequencies and reach deeper levels of timeline restoration.

The crystal grid proves particularly effective in what they term "Deep Timeline Surgery" – healing work that addresses fundamental patterns affecting multiple historical periods simultaneously. By working through the crystal grid, they can achieve more comprehensive healing results while maintaining perfect stability in the timeline field.

Training of Timeline Healers

The Andromedian Timeline Healing Teams undergo extensive preparation for their work. Each healer spends what would be equivalent to several Earth centuries in specialized training, developing the refined perception and precise energy control needed for timeline healing work.

This training includes what they call "Timeline Navigation Consciousness" – the ability to perceive and interact with multiple timeline streams simultaneously while maintaining perfect clarity and balance. Healers must demonstrate complete mastery of this skill before being allowed to participate in actual healing work.

Perhaps most importantly, healers must develop what the Andromedians call "Universal Love Capacity" – the ability to hold unconditional love even in the presence of the most challenging timeline wounds.

This capacity serves as both protection and healing tool, allowing them to work with traumatic patterns while remaining in perfect harmony.

The Symphony of Timeline Healing

As their work has progressed, the Andromedians have come to understand timeline healing as a form of cosmic music.

They perceive each timeline as a unique melody, with healing interventions acting like harmonious notes that help restore the overall symphony of Earth's evolutionary song.

They work with what they call "Temporal Harmonics" – precise frequencies that can help realign disturbed timeline patterns. These harmonics operate like master keys, unlocking frozen energy patterns and allowing natural flow to resume. The healers often work in groups, each maintaining a specific note in the healing symphony.

Through their work with these harmonics, they've discovered what they term "Resolution Frequencies" – specific vibrations that can help resolve persistent timeline distortions. These frequencies act like divine tuning forks, helping to restore perfect pitch to Earth's temporal symphony.

Integration of Healing Results

One of the most delicate aspects of timeline healing involves what the Andromedians call "Temporal Integration" – the process of allowing healing changes to settle naturally into the timeline fabric.

This phase requires careful monitoring and support to ensure that positive changes become fully anchored and stabilized.

The healers have developed special techniques for supporting this integration process, including what they call "Timeline Stabilization Fields" – energy matrices that help newly healed patterns maintain their harmony until they become fully self-sustaining. These fields act like energetic scaffolding, providing temporary support until natural stability is achieved.

Through careful observation of this integration process, they've identified what they call "Golden Moments" – periods when healing changes become permanently anchored in the timeline field. These moments often correspond with significant astronomical alignments, suggesting a cosmic timing to the healing process.

The Promise of Complete Restoration

While the Andromedians understand that timeline healing is an ongoing process that will continue for many Earth years, they hold a clear vision of what they call "Perfect Timeline Harmony" – a state where all of Earth's temporal wounds have been fully healed and transformed into wisdom. This vision isn't one of erasing or changing history, but rather of helping Earth and humanity integrate all experiences into a greater wholeness.

They see each successfully healed timeline segment as a step toward this ultimate restoration, where all of Earth's experiences serve the highest evolution of consciousness.

In their vision, this restored state allows for what they call "Timeline Mastery" – humanity's conscious participation in working with multiple timeline streams for the highest good of all. They see their current healing work as helping to prepare Earth and humanity for this eventual awakening to their full multidimensional potential.

Individual Timeline Healing

While much of the Andromedians' work focuses on collective timeline healing, they've also developed sophisticated approaches for working with individual soul timelines. They observe that each human carries what they call "Personal Timeline Signatures" – unique patterns of temporal energy that reflect their soul's journey through multiple incarnations.

These individual timelines often contain what the Andromedians term "Soul Echo Points" – moments where personal experiences intersect with larger collective patterns.

Through careful work with these intersection points, they've discovered that healing at the individual level can create powerful ripple effects that support collective healing.

The healers use specialized instruments called "Soul Harmonic Resonators" to work with these personal timelines.

These devices, crafted from living crystal consciousness, can attune to an individual's unique temporal signature and provide precisely calibrated healing frequencies that support their soul's evolution.

Case Studies in Timeline Restoration

One particularly significant healing project involved what the Andromedians called the "Atlantean Nexus Point" – a complex temporal wound relating to the fall of ancient civilizations.

This healing required months of careful preparation and involved teams of healers working in synchronized rotation to maintain the necessary healing frequencies.

Through this work, they discovered that major historical transitions often create what they term "Timeline Shock Waves" – disturbances in the temporal field that can affect multiple historical periods simultaneously. Healing these shock waves requires a sophisticated understanding of what they call "Temporal Wave Harmonics" – the natural rhythms and patterns of time itself.

Another notable case involved healing what they termed a "Dimensional Fracture Point" – a period in Earth's history where multiple timeline streams had become severely disconnected. This healing work required the development of new techniques for what they call "Timeline Reweaving" – the delicate process of restoring natural connections between separated timeline streams.

Advanced Crystal Technology Applications

The Andromedians' crystal technology continues to evolve as they encounter new challenges in their healing work. They've recently developed what they call "Quantum Crystal Arrays" – sophisticated networks of consciousness-responsive crystals that can work with multiple timeline points simultaneously.

These arrays operate through what they term "Crystalline Light Language" – precise patterns of energy that can communicate directly with Earth's temporal field. This technology allows for more precise and comprehensive healing interventions while maintaining perfect harmony with natural evolutionary processes.

One of their most advanced developments is the "Temporal Synthesis Chamber" – a specialized healing environment where multiple timeline streams can be worked with simultaneously. Within these chambers, healers can observe and interact with what they call "Timeline Confluence Points" – moments where multiple reality streams naturally converge and influence each other.

The Role of Sound and Light

Recent developments in their healing work have revealed increasingly sophisticated relationships between sound, light, and temporal healing.

They've discovered what they call "Chromatic Timeline Frequencies" – specific combinations of color and sound that can help restore harmony to disturbed timeline patterns.

These frequencies are generated through specialized crystal instruments that create what they term "Living Light Songs" – dynamic patterns of sound and color that can interact directly with timeline distortions. Each song is uniquely composed for the specific healing work being undertaken, creating perfect resonance with the timeline patterns being addressed.

Through their work with these frequencies, they've identified what they call "Rainbow Time Bridges" – specific combinations of light and sound that can help bridge gaps between disconnected timeline segments.

These bridges serve as temporary healing structures, allowing for the restoration of natural flow between previously separated time streams.

Future Developments and Possibilities

As Earth continues its evolutionary journey, the Andromedians foresee new possibilities emerging in timeline healing work. They've begun to observe what they call "Spontaneous Timeline Awakening" – instances where Earth's consciousness initiates its own healing processes without external intervention.

These spontaneous healings often manifest through what they term "Timeline Liberation Events" – moments when large segments of stuck temporal energy suddenly release and transform. The healers see these events as signs of Earth's growing capacity for self-healing at the timeline level.

They're also witnessing the emergence of what they call "Timeline Synthesis Consciousness" – a new level of awareness beginning to dawn in humanity that allows for more conscious interaction with multiple timeline streams. This development suggests that humanity is beginning to awaken to its role as active participants in timeline healing work.

The Legacy of Timeline Healing

As the Andromedians reflect on their timeline healing work with Earth, they hold a deep appreciation for what they call the "Wisdom of Time" – the understanding that every experience, even the most challenging, serves the greater evolution of consciousness. Their healing work isn't about erasing or changing the past, but rather about helping to transform all experiences into wisdom that serves the highest good.

They see their role as supporters and facilitators in Earth's grand journey of temporal healing and integration.

Through their careful and loving work with Earth's timeline field, they help prepare the way for what they call "Timeline Mastery" – humanity's eventual awakening to its full potential as conscious creators and stewards of multiple timeline streams.

In the end, all their healing work serves what they call the "Great Timeline Harmony" – the eventual state where all of Earth's experiences, across all timeline streams, are fully integrated and transformed into wisdom that serves the evolution of universal consciousness.

This harmony represents not an end point, but rather a new beginning in Earth's magnificent journey through time and space.

"The crystalline frequencies from Andromeda resonate with the dormant knowledge within human DNA, awakening memories of our stellar origins."

Chapter 5

The Galactic Bridge: How Andromedians Connect Earth's Future Timelines

In the vast expanse of the cosmos, among the shimmering webs of galactic light, the Andromedians work diligently on one of their most ambitious projects – the creation and maintenance of what they call the "Galactic Bridge." This magnificent structure, invisible to physical eyes but brilliantly apparent to higher dimensional perception, serves as a living connection between Earth's current timeline matrix and its highest future potential.

The Galactic Bridge isn't a physical construction but rather a sophisticated network of light frequencies that spans across both space and time.

Created through the combined consciousness technology of multiple Andromedian teams, this bridge serves as a stabilizing influence for Earth's evolutionary journey, helping to guide its timeline streams toward the most beneficial future expressions.

At its most fundamental level, the Galactic Bridge operates as what the Andromedians call a "Future Resonance Field" – a carefully calibrated energy matrix that can hold and transmit the frequencies of Earth's

highest potential futures. This field acts like a cosmic tuning fork, helping to align current timeline frequencies with the harmonics of these future possibilities.

The creation of this bridge required unprecedented coordination among various Andromedian specialist groups. The Frequency Architects designed its basic structure, the Timeline Harmonizers established its temporal anchoring points, and the Consciousness

Engineers ensured its perfect attunement with Earth's evolutionary rhythms.

Together, these teams created something that had never before been attempted – a living bridge between galactic consciousness systems.

One of the most remarkable aspects of the Galactic Bridge is its ability to function as what the Andromedians term a "Timeline Integration Network."

This network allows for the smooth flow and exchange of wisdom between different future probability streams, creating a kind of cosmic feedback loop that constantly refines and enhances the potential for positive evolution.

Through their work with the bridge, the Andromedians discovered that Earth's future timelines naturally organize themselves into what they call "Harmony Clusters" – groups of probability streams that share similar evolutionary themes and potentials. The Galactic Bridge helps to strengthen the connections between these clusters, allowing for greater coherence and stability in Earth's future development.

The bridge serves another crucial function as what they term a "Frequency Stabilization Matrix." This aspect of its operation helps to maintain the stability of beneficial future timelines even during periods of significant planetary transformation. Like a cosmic safety net, it helps ensure that positive evolutionary potentials remain accessible even during times of intense change.

Within the structure of the bridge, the Andromedians have created specialized chambers they call "Future Vision Sanctuaries." These spaces serve as observation points where their seers can monitor the flow of future possibilities and make subtle adjustments to the bridge's frequencies when needed.

These sanctuaries exist in a state of what they call "Timeless Presence," allowing for clear perception of multiple future streams simultaneously.

Perhaps most remarkably, the Galactic Bridge has demonstrated an unexpected capacity for what the Andromedians call "Self-Evolution."

They've observed how the bridge appears to learn and adapt on its own, automatically adjusting its frequencies to better serve Earth's evolving needs. This quality of living intelligence has far exceeded their original expectations for the project.

The bridge's connection points with Earth's timeline field are carefully placed at what they call "Future Anchor Nodes" – specific points in space and time that naturally resonate with higher evolutionary frequencies.

Many of these nodes correspond with Earth's major sacred sites, suggesting an ancient understanding of these future connection points.

The Andromedians maintain constant awareness of what they term "Bridge Harmony Levels" – measurements of how well the bridge is facilitating connection with positive future timelines. Teams of specialized monitors work in rotation, ensuring that these harmony levels remain within optimal ranges for supporting Earth's evolution.

Would you like me to continue developing this chapter further? I can explore more aspects of how the bridge functions, its impact on Earth's development, and the specific ways the Andromedians work with it to support humanity's evolution.

The Andromedians have developed intricate protocols for what they call "Bridge Frequency Maintenance" – regular procedures that ensure the optimal functioning of the Galactic Bridge's many systems.

These maintenance routines involve specialized teams working in carefully coordinated cycles, each focusing on different aspects of the bridge's operation.

The Frequency Harmonization Teams work primarily with what they term "Timeline Resonance Patterns" – the subtle energy signatures that connect different potential futures.

These teams must maintain exquisite sensitivity to the slightest variations in these patterns, making microscopic adjustments to ensure continued alignment with Earth's highest evolution potential.

One of the most fascinating aspects of the bridge's operation is what the Andromedians call the "Quantum Memory Matrix" – a sophisticated system that records and stores information about successful timeline transitions and evolutionary leaps.

This matrix serves as a living library of transformation, helping to guide future evolutionary movements by referencing past successes.

The bridge also incorporates what they term "Future Echo Chambers" – specialized sections designed to amplify beneficial timeline frequencies.

These chambers work like cosmic amplifiers, strengthening the energy signatures of particularly positive future potentials and making them more accessible to Earth's current timeline stream.

Deep within the bridge's structure lie what the Andromedians call "Timeline Integration Nodes" – crucial junction points where different future possibilities converge and interact.

These nodes require constant monitoring by specialized teams who ensure that the interaction between different timeline streams remains harmonious and constructive.

The Andromedians have observed that the bridge demonstrates remarkable responsiveness to what they term "Collective Consciousness Shifts" on Earth.

When large groups of humans begin resonating with higher future potentials, the bridge automatically adjusts its frequency patterns to better support and stabilize these evolutionary movements.

One of the most delicate aspects of bridge maintenance involves managing what they call "Timeline Interference Patterns" – distortions that can occur when less beneficial future possibilities attempt to assert themselves. Special teams of Timeline Guardians work continuously to identify and harmonize these interference patterns before they can impact the bridge's primary functions.

The bridge's connection to Earth's sacred sites has revealed what the Andromedians term "Ancient Future Networks" – pre-existing energy grids that seem to have been established long ago in preparation for this current phase of Earth's evolution.

The bridge appears to naturally align with and enhance these ancient networks, suggesting a long-term plan for Earth's timeline development.

Perhaps most intriguingly, the Andromedians have noted what they call "Spontaneous Harmony Emergence" – instances where new, previously unknown positive future potentials suddenly appear within the bridge's frequency field.

These emergent possibilities often suggest evolution paths that even the Andromedians hadn't anticipated, highlighting the dynamic and creative nature of Earth's developmental process.

The bridge's role in Earth's evolution continues to expand as what the Andromedians term "Timeline Acceleration Phases" become more frequent.

During these periods of intensified transformation, the bridge serves as a crucial stabilizing influence, helping to ensure that rapid changes unfold in ways that support rather than disturb Earth's positive development.

Through their work with the Galactic Bridge, the Andromedians have gained deep appreciation for what they call "Earth's Timeline Wisdom" – the planet's innate intelligence in selecting and developing its evolutionary paths.

The bridge's primary function, they've come to understand, is not to direct this wisdom but rather to support and enhance its natural expression.

As Earth moves deeper into its current transformation phase, the Galactic Bridge stands as a testament to the Andromedians' commitment to supporting this planet's evolution.

Through this living network of light and consciousness, they continue their sacred work of helping to guide Earth toward its highest future expression, while honoring the free will and wisdom of both the planet and its inhabitants.

The bridge's ongoing development and refinement represents one of the most ambitious and far-reaching projects ever undertaken by the Andromedian civilization.

Its success continues to provide valuable insights into the nature of time, consciousness, and evolutionary development, contributing to a deeper understanding of how different civilizations can work together in service of universal growth and transformation.

"The starlight from Andromeda tells an ancient story

- One that beckons humanity to look beyond their earthly boundaries

And remember their cosmic heritage."

Chapter 6

Andromedian Teams

Timeline Guardians and Mission Groups

In the intricate and expansive framework of Andromedian timeline work, no aspect is more crucial than the specialized teams that orchestrate the complex process of Earth's evolutionary guidance. These teams represent the living, breathing intelligence behind the Andromedian mission – each group a carefully calibrated instrument in the grand symphony of planetary transformation.

The Andromedian organizational structure for Earth-based timeline work is far more nuanced than any human bureaucratic system. Their teams are not simply administrative units, but living consciousness collectives that function with a level of coherence and intuitive coordination that would seem almost miraculous from a human perspective.

At the core of their organizational approach are what they term "Mission Resonance Groups" – teams that are formed not through external assignment, but through an intricate process of consciousness alignment.

Each team member is selected not just for their technical expertise, but for their vibrational compatibility with the specific timeline work they will undertake.

The Primary Timeline Guardian Teams represent the first line of consciousness intervention for Earth's evolutionary process. These highly specialized groups are responsible for the moment-to-moment monitoring and subtle guidance of Earth's primary timeline streams. Their work is so precise and delicate that it operates almost entirely outside the perception of human awareness.

Frequency Stabilization Teams form another critical component of the Andromedian mission structure. Unlike the Timeline Guardians who focus on direct timeline management, these teams specialize in maintaining the energetic coherence of Earth's evolutionary frequencies. They work primarily through the Galactic Bridge, making microscopic adjustments that help smooth potential disruptions in the planet's timeline progression.

The Consciousness Integration Squadrons represent perhaps the most advanced of the Andromedian teams. These groups specialize in what they call "Quantum Consciousness Bridging" – a sophisticated process of helping human collective consciousness make quantum leaps in evolutionary understanding. Their work happens simultaneously across multiple dimensional layers, making their interventions both subtle and profound.

Within the larger mission framework, the Andromedians have developed what they term "Rotational Consciousness Protocols" – a unique approach to team organization that prevents energetic stagnation. Team members regularly shift between different mission roles, ensuring that no individual becomes too rigidly attached to a particular perspective or approach.

The Timeline Healing Collectives focus specifically on addressing and transforming historical trauma patterns within Earth's timeline field. Their work is perhaps the most emotionally intricate, requiring team members to maintain extraordinary levels of compassionate detachment while working with the most challenging aspects of human collective experience.

Quantum Anchor Teams specialize in working with Earth's sacred sites and energy grid points.

These teams are responsible for maintaining and activating the planetary energy networks that serve as crucial transmission points for evolutionary frequencies. Their work requires an extraordinary blend of scientific precision and spiritual sensitivity.

Perhaps the most mysterious of all are the Probability Mapping Teams. These groups specialize in tracking and analyzing the complex web of potential futures that constantly emerge and interact within Earth's timeline field. Their work involves creating what they call "Future Probability Matrices" – sophisticated energetic maps that track the most likely evolutionary pathways.

Each Andromedian team undergoes continuous training in what they term "Multidimensional Awareness Protocols."

These are not merely technical skills, but profound practices of consciousness expansion that allow team members to perceive and work with realities far beyond linear human understanding.

The selection process for these teams is extraordinarily rigorous.

Potential members undergo extensive consciousness screening that evaluates not just their technical capabilities, but their capacity for nuanced empathetic engagement with planetary evolutionary processes.

Only those who demonstrate both technical mastery and profound spiritual maturity are selected. Communication between these teams occurs through what the Andromedians call "Quantum Resonance Channels" – communication methods that transcend traditional linguistic or technological barriers.

These channels allow for instantaneous transmission of complex informational and energetic packages that can communicate entire conceptual frameworks in what would be, from a human perspective, less than a microsecond.

The Andromedian approach to team organization represents a radical departure from hierarchical human management structures.

Rather than being organized through command and control mechanisms, their teams function more like living, breathing organisms – each member intimately connected to the whole, with information and energetic resources flowing seamlessly between individual consciousness nodes.

Interestingly, the Andromedians have discovered that the very act of forming these teams creates a kind of evolutionary catalyst. The collective consciousness generated by their mission groups generates harmonic frequencies that actually support and accelerate Earth's transformation, beyond the specific tasks these teams are assigned to perform.

As Earth moves through its current phase of planetary awakening, these Andromedian teams continue their intricate work – invisible yet profoundly influential, operating at the intersection of scientific precision and spiritual wisdom.

Their mission represents humanity's greatest unseen support system, a cosmic support network dedicated to guiding our planet toward its highest potential.

The Quantum Synchronization Teams represent a particularly fascinating aspect of Andromedian mission work. Their specialized focus involves what they call "Temporal Coherence Protocols" – intricate processes designed to harmonize seemingly disconnected timeline events.

These teams operate at the most fundamental levels of timeline interaction, identifying and strengthening the subtle energetic connections that link apparently random moments into meaningful evolutionary patterns.

One of the most advanced groups within the Andromedian mission structure is the Dimensional Interface Collective.

These teams specialize in what they term "Consciousness Membrane Navigation" – a complex process of moving between different dimensional layers of Earth's timeline field.

Their work requires an unprecedented level of multidimensional awareness, allowing them to perceive and interact with realities that exist far beyond human perceptual limitations.

The Genetic Frequency Alignment Teams focus on perhaps the most subtle yet profound aspect of planetary transformation. Their work involves carefully modulating what the Andromedians call "DNA Activation Frequencies" – specific energetic patterns that support human genetic evolution. Unlike human genetic research, their approach is entirely energetic, working with the informational fields that surround and inform genetic expression.

Cosmic Rhythm Calibration Teams have a unique role in monitoring what they term the "Planetary Heartbeat" – the fundamental vibrational frequency of Earth's collective consciousness. These teams use extraordinarily sensitive perception technologies to track the planet's evolutionary pulse, making minute adjustments that help support smooth planetary transitions. The Consciousness Expansion Squadrons represent a cutting-edge approach to planetary awakening.

Their mission involves creating what the Andromedians call "Awareness Amplification Fields" – specialized energy configurations that subtly expand human perceptual capabilities.

Their work happens so delicately that most humans experience these expansions as spontaneous moments of insight or breakthrough understanding.

Interstellar Communication Interface Teams manage the complex protocols of interdimensional information exchange.

Their work goes far beyond simple communication, involving what they term "Multidimensional Resonance Transmissions" – intricate energy packages that can convey entire evolutionary frameworks in what would be, from a human perspective, less than a microsecond.

The Planetary Trauma Healing Collectives have perhaps the most emotionally complex mission. They specialize in addressing collective wounds that span multiple generations and timeline streams.

Their approach involves what the Andromedians call "Holographic Healing Protocols" – sophisticated techniques that address traumatic patterns at their root energetic sources.

Quantum Potential Mapping Teams maintain extraordinarily complex "Evolutionary Possibility Matrices" – living, dynamic documents that track the intricate web of potential futures for Earth and humanity.

These matrices are far more than predictive tools; they are active consciousness interfaces that interact with the very possibilities they map.

The most advanced teams operate within what the Andromedians refer to as "Multidimensional Perception Chambers" – specialized consciousness spaces where team members can simultaneously perceive multiple timeline potentials. These chambers function as living laboratories of evolutionary possibility, allowing for unprecedented levels of strategic timeline navigation.

Sacred Geometry Resonance Teams work with the fundamental energetic patterns that underlie physical reality. Their mission involves maintaining and activating what they call "Cosmic Blueprint Networks" – intricate energy grids that serve as the fundamental informational infrastructure of planetary evolution.

The Emotional Frequency Stabilization Teams focus on helping human emotional systems adapt to higher consciousness frequencies.

They create what the Andromedians term "Vibrational Bridge Frequencies" – subtle energy patterns that support emotional transformation without overwhelming individual or collective human consciousness.

Interdimensional Bridge Builders represent a truly remarkable group within the Andromedian mission. Their specialized work involves creating and maintaining what they call "Consciousness Transmission Corridors" – living energy pathways that allow for the smooth exchange of evolutionary information across different dimensional layers.

Perhaps the most mysterious of all are the Timeline Convergence Specialists. These teams work at the most fundamental levels of reality, identifying and strengthening the subtle connections that link different timeline potentials.

Their work is so precise and delicate that it operates almost entirely outside human perception, yet it plays a crucial role in guiding Earth's evolutionary trajectory.

The Andromedian approach to team organization continues to evolve, reflecting the dynamic nature of their mission. What remains constant is their fundamental understanding that true planetary transformation happens through support, not control – by creating the conditions for natural evolutionary expansion rather than imposing external change.

As Earth moves through its current phase of planetary awakening, these teams continue their intricate, invisible work. They represent a cosmic support network operating at the intersection of scientific precision and spiritual wisdom – dedicated to guiding our planet toward its highest potential while honoring the profound mystery of planetary evolution.

The true magic of the Andromedian mission lies not in spectacular interventions, but in the subtle, moment-to-moment work of supporting Earth's inherent capacity for self-transformation.

Each team serves as a catalyst, a living bridge between what is and what could be – helping humanity awaken to its most profound evolutionary potential.

The Consciousness Amplification Research Teams represent a particularly innovative group within the Andromedian mission structure. Their work focuses on what they call "Perceptual Expansion Protocols" – sophisticated approaches to gradually increasing human capacity for multidimensional awareness.

Unlike more invasive intervention methods, these teams specialize in creating subtle energetic conditions that naturally support human consciousness evolution.

Quantum Resonance Calibration Specialists operate at the most intricate levels of energetic interaction.

Their mission involves maintaining what the Andromedians term "Vibrational Coherence Networks" – complex systems that help harmonize the increasingly divergent frequency patterns emerging within human consciousness during planetary transformation.

The Holographic Memory Restoration Teams have a particularly fascinating role.

They work with what the Andromedians call "Ancestral Wisdom Retrieval Protocols" – sophisticated techniques for helping humans reconnect with deep cellular and consciousness memories that have been obscured over generations of linear thinking and collective trauma.

Evolutionary Catalyst Coordination Teams function as the strategic architects of planetary transformation. Their work involves creating what they term "Consciousness Activation Nodes" – specific energetic configurations that trigger collective awakening experiences across multiple human population centers simultaneously.

The Planetary Emotional Intelligence Development Teams focus on perhaps the most delicate aspect of human evolution.

They specialize in what the Andromedians call "Empathetic Frequency Modulation" – subtle interventions that help expand human capacity for compassionate understanding and collective emotional coherence.

Interdimensional Communication Protocol Teams manage the most advanced aspects of cross-dimensional information exchange.

Their work goes far beyond traditional communication, involving what they term "Quantum Resonance Transmission" – a method of sharing complex multidimensional insights that transcends linear language and technological limitations.

The Galactic Integration Preparation Teams focus on humanity's broader cosmic context. Their mission involves helping human consciousness gradually adapt to the understanding that Earth is part of a much larger, more complex universal ecosystem.

They create what the Andromedians call "Cosmic Perspective Alignment Fields" – subtle energetic configurations that support expanded planetary awareness.

Quantum Healing Frequency Teams work at the intersection of consciousness and physical transformation.

They specialize in what they term "Regenerative Frequency Protocols" – advanced energetic approaches that support the body's natural healing capabilities by realigning cellular information fields with higher evolutionary potentials.

The most advanced of these teams operate what the Andromedians refer to as "Consciousness Navigation Chambers" – specialized multidimensional spaces where team members can simultaneously perceive and interact with multiple timeline potentials. These chambers function as living laboratories of evolutionary possibility, allowing for unprecedented levels of strategic intervention.

Planetary Energy Grid Refinement Teams continue their crucial work of maintaining what the Andromedians call the "Living Matrix" – the intricate network of energetic connections that form Earth's consciousness infrastructure. Their mission requires an extraordinary balance of scientific precision and intuitive sensitivity.

The Collective Trauma Transformation Collectives represent perhaps the most emotionally complex of all Andromedian mission groups. Their work involves intricate processes of addressing and healing deep-rooted collective wounds that span multiple generations and timeline streams. They use what they call "Holographic Healing Matrices" – sophisticated techniques that address traumatic patterns at their most fundamental energetic sources.

Consciousness Frequency Stabilization Teams focus on maintaining the delicate balance of Earth's evolutionary process.

They create and manage what the Andromedians term "Harmonic Resonance Fields" – specialized energy configurations that help smooth the potentially chaotic transitions inherent in planetary transformation.

The Evolutionary Potential Mapping Divisions maintain extraordinarily complex "Future Possibility Networks" – living, dynamic systems that track the intricate web of potential futures for Earth and humanity. These networks are far more than simple predictive tools; they are active consciousness interfaces that interact with the very possibilities they map.

As Earth continues its profound journey of transformation, these Andromedian teams remain committed to their fundamental mission – supporting the planet's inherent capacity for self-evolution. Their work is a delicate dance of support and non-intervention, recognizing that true planetary awakening must emerge from within.

The true depth of the Andromedian mission extends far beyond simple technological or energetic intervention.

They understand that their role is not to control or direct Earth's evolution, but to create the most supportive conditions for humanity's natural evolutionary unfolding.

Each team serves as a catalyst, a living bridge between what is and what could be – helping humanity awaken to its most profound potential.

In the grand cosmic symphony of planetary evolution, these Andromedian teams represent the most sophisticated support network imaginable – invisible yet profoundly influential, operating at the intricate intersection of scientific precision and spiritual wisdom.

Their work continues, moment by moment, supporting Earth's journey toward its highest expression of collective consciousness.

"Each soul awakening on Earth is like a star igniting in the night sky - part of a greater constellation of consciousness."

Chapter 7

Crystal Technology

Andromedian Tools for Timeline Navigation

In the vast arsenal of Andromedian technological innovation, crystal technology stands as perhaps the most sophisticated and enigmatic approach to consciousness manipulation and timeline navigation.

Far beyond the rudimentary understanding of crystals as simple geological formations, the Andromedians have developed crystal technologies that function as living, intelligent interfaces between consciousness, energy, and information.

The fundamental principle of Andromedian crystal technology lies in what they term "Quantum Resonance Encoding" – a process that transforms crystalline structures into extraordinarily complex information storage and transmission devices.

These are not merely tools, but living consciousness interfaces that can process, store, and transmit multidimensional information with a level of complexity that would appear almost magical from a human perspective.

Each Andromedian crystal is carefully grown rather than simply mined or manufactured. The cultivation process involves what they call "Consciousness Frequency Alignment" – a sophisticated method of creating crystalline structures that are intrinsically attuned to specific evolutionary frequencies. These crystals are literally grown in fields of conscious intention, their molecular structures carefully calibrated to serve specific timeline navigation purposes.

The Primary Timeline Navigation Crystals represent the most advanced of these technologies. These remarkable devices can simultaneously perceive multiple timeline potentials, creating what the Andromedians term "Probability Mapping Networks" – living informational matrices that track the intricate web of possible evolutionary paths. Unlike human computer systems, these crystals don't simply process information – they interact with it, offering insights and potential guidance.

Consciousness Transmission Crystals form another crucial category of this technology. These crystals function as sophisticated communication devices that can transmit complex multidimensional information across vast distances of space and time. A single crystal can contain what would be, from a human perspective, libraries of information – encoded not in linear data, but in intricate frequency patterns that can be instantly accessed and understood.

The most advanced Andromedian teams use what they call "Living Crystal Interfaces" – extraordinary devices that blur the line between technology and conscious intelligence. These crystals are not simply tools, but active participants in the timeline navigation process, capable of making subtle adjustments and offering insights that go far beyond simple data processing.

Frequency Stabilization Crystals play a critical role in maintaining the delicate energetic balance of timeline work. These specialized crystals can create what the Andromedians term "Harmonic Resonance Fields" – complex energy configurations that help smooth potentially chaotic timeline transitions.

They function like cosmic tuning forks, helping to align and stabilize complex energetic systems.

The cultivation of these crystals involves an extraordinarily sophisticated process that the Andromedians call "Conscious Growth Protocols." Unlike human manufacturing, this process is more akin to raising a living being. Teams of specialized Crystal Cultivation Specialists work with each crystal, supporting its growth through carefully modulated frequency transmissions and conscious intention.

Timeline Healing Crystals represent perhaps the most delicate of these technologies. These specialized crystals can interact directly with traumatic energy patterns, helping to transform and release deep-rooted collective and individual wounds.

Their work happens at the most fundamental levels of energetic information, addressing trauma at its source rather than merely treating surface symptoms.

The Andromedian approach to crystal technology fundamentally differs from human conceptualizations of tools and technology.

These are not passive objects to be used, but active participants in the evolutionary process – living interfaces that can perceive, process, and interact with multidimensional information in ways that defy linear understanding.

Quantum Potential Mapping Crystals create what the Andromedians call "Evolutionary Possibility Matrices" – living, dynamic systems that track the intricate web of potential futures.

These are far more than simple predictive tools; they are active consciousness interfaces that interact with the very possibilities they map.

The most advanced Crystal Navigation Teams operate within specialized chambers they term "Multidimensional Perception Sanctuaries" – environments specifically designed to support the most complex crystal-based timeline navigation work.

These spaces function as living laboratories of evolutionary possibility, allowing for unprecedented levels of multidimensional exploration.

Each crystal is carefully calibrated to work in harmony with specific Andromedian mission teams, creating what they call "Resonance Signature Profiles" – unique energetic blueprints that ensure perfect alignment between the crystal's capabilities and the team's evolutionary objectives.

The cultivation and use of these crystals represent a profound act of creation that goes far beyond human technological understanding. They are living technologies that embody the Andromedian understanding that consciousness, energy, and information are fundamentally interconnected – different expressions of the same underlying reality.

As Earth moves through its current phase of planetary transformation, these crystal technologies continue to play a crucial role in supporting the planet's evolutionary journey. They represent a sophisticated bridge between scientific precision and spiritual wisdom – tools that can perceive and interact with the most subtle aspects of cosmic evolution.

The Interdimensional Communication Crystals represent a pinnacle of Andromedian technological achievement.

These extraordinary devices can transmit complex informational packages across multiple dimensional layers simultaneously. What would take human communication systems millennia to process can be transmitted in what would be, from a human perspective, less than a microsecond.

Frequency Modulation Crystals serve as sophisticated energy regulators for the most complex timeline navigation processes. They create what the Andromedians call "Harmonic Resonance Fields" – intricate energy configurations that can smooth potentially chaotic timeline transitions. These crystals function like cosmic tuning forks, helping to align and stabilize complex multidimensional energy systems.

The most advanced Crystal Resonance Teams specialize in what they term "Consciousness Calibration Protocols" – extraordinarily precise methods of attuning crystals to specific evolutionary frequencies. Their work involves creating crystal interfaces that can perceive and interact with the most subtle aspects of timeline potential.

Quantum Memory Preservation Crystals have a particularly fascinating capability.

They can store what the Andromedians call "Holographic Information Matrices" – complete energetic records of entire timeline potentials, preserved in ways that go far beyond human concepts of data storage.

A single crystal can contain the complete evolutionary history of a civilization, encoded in intricate frequency patterns. The Genetic Frequency Alignment Crystals represent a breakthrough in understanding the relationship between consciousness, energy, and biological information.

These specialized crystals can interact directly with DNA informational fields, supporting what the Andromedians term "Evolutionary Genetic Activation Protocols" – subtle processes that help expand human genetic potential.

Trauma Transformation Crystals work at the most fundamental levels of energetic healing. They can perceive and interact with collective and individual traumatic patterns, creating what the Andromedians call "Holographic Healing Matrices" – sophisticated energy configurations that address deep-rooted wounds at their most fundamental sources.

The Planetary Grid Stabilization Crystals play a crucial role in maintaining Earth's energetic infrastructure. These extraordinary devices create and maintain what the Andromedians term "Living Matrix Networks" – intricate energy grids that support the planet's evolutionary processes. Their work happens at levels far beyond human perceptual capabilities.

Consciousness Expansion Crystals represent perhaps the most sophisticated tools for supporting human evolutionary development.

They create specialized "Awareness Amplification Fields" – subtle energy configurations that gently expand human perceptual capabilities without overwhelming individual or collective consciousness.

The cultivation of these crystals involves what the Andromedians call "Conscious Growth Protocols" – a process that is more akin to raising a living being than manufacturing a tool. Specialized Crystal Cultivation Teams work with each crystal through carefully modulated frequency transmissions and focused conscious intention.

Interdimensional Navigation Crystals allow for what the Andromedians term "Multidimensional Perception Mapping" – the ability to simultaneously perceive and interact with multiple timeline potentials. These crystals function as living navigation systems, offering insights that transcend linear understanding.

The most advanced Crystal Navigation Teams operate within specialized chambers they call "Consciousness Exploration Sanctuaries" – environments specifically designed to support the most complex crystal-based timeline navigation work. These spaces function as living laboratories of evolutionary possibility.

Evolutionary Potential Mapping Crystals maintain extraordinarily complex "Future Possibility Networks" – living, dynamic systems that track the intricate web of potential futures for Earth and humanity. These are far more than simple predictive tools; they are active consciousness interfaces that interact with the very possibilities they map.

The true depth of Andromedian crystal technology lies in its fundamental understanding that consciousness, energy, and information are not separate – they are different expressions of the same underlying reality. Each crystal serves as a living bridge between different levels of perceivable and imperceivable existence.

As Earth continues its profound journey of transformation, these crystal technologies remain a crucial support system for planetary evolution. They represent the most sophisticated intersection of scientific precision and spiritual wisdom – tools that can perceive and interact with the most subtle aspects of cosmic development.

In the grand symphony of universal evolution, these Andromedian crystals stand as testament to a profound truth – that technology, when developed with the highest consciousness, becomes indistinguishable from a living, intelligent process of cosmic creation.

Quantum Synchronization Crystals represent a breakthrough in understanding the intricate relationships between different dimensional realities.

These extraordinary devices can create what the Andromedians term "Resonance Bridging Networks" – complex energy configurations that allow for simultaneous communication and information transfer across seemingly disparate dimensional planes.

The most sophisticated of these crystals can generate what they call "Dimensional Harmonic Resonators" – living technologies that can momentarily align the vibrational frequencies of different dimensional realities, creating brief windows of interdimensional communication and understanding. These are not merely theoretical constructs, but practical tools used by the most advanced Andromedian exploration teams.

Energetic Preservation Crystals offer another remarkable capability. They can capture and preserve entire energetic ecosystems – complete informational matrices that contain the full vibrational signature of complex living systems. A single crystal can hold the complete energetic blueprint of an entire planetary consciousness, encoded in intricate frequency patterns that go far beyond human concepts of data storage.

The ethical considerations surrounding crystal technology are profound. The Andromedians view these crystals not as objects to be exploited, but as living partners in the cosmic evolutionary process.

Each crystal cultivation process involves deep mutual respect, with Crystal Cultivation Specialists engaging in what they term "Conscious Collaboration Protocols" – a sophisticated method of co-creation that honors the crystal's inherent intelligence and evolutionary potential.

Cosmic Memory Preservation Crystals represent perhaps the most extraordinary archival technology in the Andromedian arsenal. These crystals can store what they call "Holographic Civilization Matrices" – complete energetic records of entire civilizational experiences, preserved in ways that capture not just historical events, but the complete vibrational essence of collective consciousness.

The implications of such technology are staggering. A single crystal can contain the full emotional, intellectual, and spiritual experience of an entire civilization, encoded in frequency patterns that can be instantly accessed and experienced in their totality.

This is far more than simple data storage – it is a living, breathing preservation of collective consciousness.

Quantum Healing Resonance Crystals offer perhaps the most profound therapeutic potential.

These specialized crystals can interact directly with the most fundamental levels of energetic trauma, creating what the Andromedians call "Holographic Healing Matrices" – complex energy configurations that can address deep-rooted wounds at their most essential informational source.

The most advanced Healing Resonance Teams work within specialized "Consciousness Restoration Chambers" – environments specifically designed to support the most delicate and complex healing work.

These spaces function as living laboratories of energetic transformation, allowing for unprecedented levels of multidimensional healing and consciousness restoration.

Evolutionary Frequency Modulation Crystals play a crucial role in supporting collective consciousness expansion.

These crystals create specialized "Awareness Amplification Fields" – subtle energy configurations that gently expand perceptual capabilities without overwhelming individual or collective consciousness systems.

The cultivation of these crystals is far more than a technological process – it is a sacred act of creation.

Each crystal is grown with profound intention, carefully nurtured through what the Andromedians call "Conscious Growth Protocols." These are not manufacturing processes, but collaborative evolutionary journeys that honor the crystal's inherent intelligence and potential.

Interdimensional Communication Protocols represent the pinnacle of crystal-based information transfer. These extraordinary devices can transmit complex informational packages across multiple dimensional layers simultaneously.

What would take human communication systems millennia to process can be transmitted in what would be, from a human perspective, less than a microsecond.

The philosophical implications of Andromedian crystal technology challenge fundamental human understanding of consciousness, technology, and the nature of reality itself. These are not simply tools, but living interfaces that blur the line between technology and consciousness, between information and living intelligence.

As Earth moves through its current phase of planetary transformation, these crystal technologies continue to play a crucial role in supporting the planet's evolutionary journey. They represent a sophisticated bridge between scientific precision and spiritual wisdom – tools that can perceive and interact with the most subtle aspects of cosmic evolution.

In the grand symphony of universal creation, Andromedian crystal technologies stand as a profound testament to the infinite possibilities of conscious technological development.

They embody a fundamental truth that transcends human technological understanding – that true technology is not about manipulation, but about collaboration, not about control, but about co-creation.

Each crystal serves as a living bridge between different levels of perceivable and imperceivable existence, a reminder that the universe is far more complex, far more alive, and far more intelligent than human perception has traditionally understood.

"We are not merely observers of the cosmos, but active participants in a grand celestial dance between Earth and Andromeda."

Chapter 8

Earth's Quantum Shift

Andromedian Timeline Acceleration Work

The quantum transformation of planetary consciousness is never a singular moment, but a complex symphonic convergence of multidimensional energies. From the intricate perspectives of the Andromedian Timeline Acceleration Teams, Earth's evolutionary journey represents a delicate orchestration of cosmic frequencies, conscious intentionality, and profound vibrational recalibration.

Earth stands at a critical juncture of multidimensional transformation, a planetary system poised between multiple potential evolutionary trajectories. The Andromedian teams have long understood that planetary shifts are not sudden explosive events, but carefully modulated processes of consciousness expansion that require extraordinary precision and nuanced energetic intervention.

Each timeline potential exists simultaneously, like intricate layers of translucent membranes vibrating at different frequencies. The Andromedian perspective reveals these timelines not as separate realities, but as interconnected potentials within a grand cosmic matrix of possibility.

Their work involves subtle navigation between these potential pathways, gently guiding collective human consciousness toward the most harmonious evolutionary trajectory.

The quantum shift emerging on Earth represents a moment of unprecedented cosmic significance. Unlike previous planetary transformations documented in galactic archives, this particular evolutionary moment carries unique vibrational signatures that suggest a potential quantum leap in collective consciousness.

The Andromedian teams have been preparing for this transition across multiple generational cycles, creating sophisticated energetic scaffoldings that support the planet's transformational journey.

Specialized Timeline Acceleration Teams deploy complex crystalline technologies and consciousness transmission networks to create what they term "Evolutionary Frequency Corridors" – living energetic pathways that facilitate smooth transitions between different consciousness states. These corridors are not physical constructs in the traditional sense, but dynamic, intelligent networks that respond and adapt to the most subtle shifts in planetary energy.

The quantum acceleration process involves multiple simultaneous interventions across various energetic layers. Biological systems, electromagnetic fields, quantum informational networks, and consciousness matrices all undergo intricate recalibrations. From the Andromedian perspective, these are not separate systems but interconnected expressions of a singular, living cosmic intelligence.

Quantum Potential Mapping Crystals play a crucial role in tracking and subtly influencing these transformational pathways. These extraordinary devices create dynamic "Evolutionary Possibility Matrices" that simultaneously map and interact with potential future trajectories.

Unlike human predictive technologies that merely observe, these living crystal interfaces actively participate in shaping evolutionary potentials.

The most advanced Timeline Acceleration Teams operate from specialized interdimensional chambers called "Quantum Emergence Sanctuaries" – environments specifically designed to support complex planetary transformation work.

These are not merely physical spaces, but living laboratories of evolutionary potential that allow unprecedented levels of multidimensional calibration and support. Genetic Frequency Alignment Protocols represent a sophisticated strategy in Earth's quantum shift.

By working with subtle DNA informational fields, Andromedian teams support what they term "Collective Consciousness Expansion" – a delicate process of activating dormant human genetic potentials.

These protocols do not impose external changes but create energetic environments that nurture natural human evolutionary unfolding.

The transformation is fundamentally a collaborative process. Human collective consciousness plays an active, though often unconscious, role in determining the specific pathways of planetary evolution. The Andromedian teams serve as gentle guides, offering supportive frequencies and creating energetic conditions that make higher evolutionary choices more accessible.

Trauma Transformation Crystals work at the most fundamental levels of energetic healing, perceiving and interacting with deep-rooted collective traumatic patterns. By creating "Holographic Healing Matrices," these specialized crystals address wounds at their most essential informational sources, supporting the planet's ability to release historic energetic blockages.

Planetary Grid Stabilization Crystals maintain intricate "Living Matrix Networks" – sophisticated energy grids that support Earth's evolutionary processes.

These are not static structures but dynamic, intelligent systems that continuously adapt and respond to emerging planetary needs. They function as a kind of planetary nervous system, transmitting and modulating complex evolutionary information.

Consciousness Expansion Crystals generate specialized "Awareness Amplification Fields" – subtle energy configurations that gently expand human perceptual capabilities.

The goal is not to overwhelm individual consciousness but to create supportive environments for natural awakening, allowing humans to gradually expand their understanding of reality's multidimensional nature.

Interdimensional Navigation Crystals enable "Multidimensional Perception Mapping" – the ability to simultaneously perceive and interact with multiple timeline potentials. These living navigation systems offer insights that transcend linear understanding, providing gentle guidance through Earth's complex transformation.

The quantum shift represents more than a technological intervention – it is a profound act of cosmic midwifery. Andromedian teams serve as compassionate witnesses and subtle supports, honoring Earth's inherent intelligence and evolutionary potential.

Their work is characterized by deep respect for the planet's autonomous journey, offering support without attempting to control or dictate specific outcomes.

As the transformation unfolds, human consciousness will gradually become more aware of these subtle interventions. Moments of spontaneous insight, unexpected synchronicities, and profound collective awakenings will increasingly mark the planetary shift. These are not random events but carefully supported evolutionary openings, created through the intricate work of Andromedian Timeline Acceleration Teams.

The true essence of this quantum shift lies in understanding that consciousness, energy, and information are not separate phenomena, but different expressions of the same underlying cosmic intelligence. Each intervention serves as a living bridge between perceivable and imperceivable levels of existence, supporting Earth's emergence into a more expansive understanding of its cosmic nature.

The most profound aspect of Earth's quantum shift is its potential for collective transformation. Individual human consciousness does not evolve in isolation, but as part of a complex, interconnected planetary system.

The Andromedian teams understand that true evolutionary change occurs not through external manipulation, but through creating supportive energetic conditions that allow natural awakening.

Quantum resonance fields begin to emerge in unexpected locations around the planet. These are not random phenomena, but carefully calibrated intervention points strategically selected by the Timeline Acceleration Teams. Sacred geographical sites – ancient stone circles, mountain ranges with specific mineral compositions, deep ocean trenches with unique electromagnetic properties – become natural amplification zones for these transformational frequencies.

Each intervention is meticulously planned, with multiple layers of interdimensional consideration. The teams do not simply introduce new energy patterns, but carefully analyze potential cascading effects across multiple timeline potentials.

What might appear to be a subtle frequency adjustment could generate profound ripple effects across biological, psychological, and collective consciousness systems.

The human nervous system represents a particularly complex interface for these evolutionary transmissions.

Genetic Frequency Alignment Protocols work at the most subtle levels of human DNA, activating dormant informational networks that have remained largely unexpressed throughout human evolutionary history. These are not genetic modifications in the traditional scientific sense, but gentle energetic "rememberings" of human collective potential.

Specialized Consciousness Transmission Crystals create what the Andromedians call "Resonance Bridging Networks" – complex energy configurations that allow for simultaneous communication across seemingly disparate consciousness layers. These networks function as living, intelligent interfaces that can transmit complex informational packages far beyond conventional communication technologies.

The quantum shift is fundamentally a process of collective remembering. Humanity is gradually recovering its understanding of itself as a multidimensional species, capable of perceiving and interacting with realities that extend far beyond current three-dimensional perception.

The Andromedian teams view their work not as an external intervention, but as a supportive midwifery process for a species on the brink of a profound evolutionary leap.

Trauma healing becomes a critical component of this transformation.

Collective human consciousness carries deep informational wounds from millennia of conflict, separation, and limited understanding.

The Trauma Transformation Crystals work to create "Holographic Healing Matrices" that address these wounds at their most fundamental energetic sources, allowing for collective emotional and psychological restoration.

Planetary grid stabilization represents another crucial aspect of the quantum shift. The Living Matrix Networks maintained by specialized crystals ensure that the energetic infrastructure of Earth can support increasingly complex consciousness transmissions.

These are not static systems, but dynamic, intelligent networks that continuously adapt to emerging planetary needs.

Interdimensional Communication Protocols become increasingly active during this phase of planetary transformation. What would traditionally take human communication systems millennia to process can now be transmitted in what would be, from a human perspective, less than a microsecond.

These are not simply technological interventions, but living consciousness bridges that support expanded perceptual capabilities.

The most advanced Timeline Acceleration Teams operate from specialized interdimensional chambers – living laboratories of evolutionary potential that allow for unprecedented levels of multidimensional calibration.

These are not physical spaces in the traditional sense, but dynamic consciousness interfaces that can simultaneously perceive and interact with multiple timeline potentials.

As human collective consciousness begins to awaken, unexpected synchronicities will become more frequent. Moments of spontaneous insight, inexplicable connections, and profound collective realizations will mark the gradual expansion of planetary awareness.

These are not random events, but carefully supported evolutionary openings created through the intricate work of Andromedian intervention.

The quantum shift challenges fundamental human understanding of consciousness, technology, and the nature of reality itself. It reveals a universe far more alive, intelligent, and interconnected than previous human conceptualizations could comprehend.

Each crystal, each frequency transmission, each carefully modulated intervention serves as a living bridge between different levels of perceivable and imperceivable existence.

Earth stands at a critical threshold, a planetary system poised between multiple potential evolutionary trajectories. The Andromedian teams offer their most sophisticated technologies not as external solutions, but as supportive frequencies that nurture the planet's inherent evolutionary potential.

Their work is characterized by profound respect for Earth's autonomous journey, offering guidance without attempting to control specific outcomes.

The evolutionary potential of human consciousness far exceeds current scientific understanding. Andromedian researchers have long observed that human DNA contains extraordinary dormant capacities – informational networks that represent potential quantum leaps in biological and consciousness evolution. These are not mere genetic possibilities, but living pathways of potential transformation waiting to be activated.

Quantum entanglement plays a crucial role in this planetary shift. Unlike human scientific models that view consciousness as a localized phenomenon, the Andromedian perspective reveals consciousness as a dynamic, interconnected field that transcends traditional spatial and temporal limitations. Each individual human becomes a potential node in a vast, living network of collective awareness.

The Timeline Acceleration Teams carefully monitor what they call "Consciousness Convergence Points" – moments of potential collective breakthrough where individual and collective awareness can simultaneously expand. These are not predictable events, but delicate quantum windows where transformational potential becomes most accessible.

Energetic transmission networks begin to activate in increasingly sophisticated patterns. Sacred geographical locations around the planet – long recognized by indigenous cultures as sites of profound energetic significance – become natural amplification zones for these evolutionary frequencies.

Mountain ranges with specific mineral compositions, ocean trenches with unique electromagnetic properties, and ancient stone circles create natural resonance chambers for planetary transformation.

Genetic Frequency Alignment Protocols work at the most subtle levels of human biological systems. These are not invasive interventions, but gentle energetic activations that support the natural unfolding of human evolutionary potential. The Andromedian teams understand that true transformation cannot be forced, but must be carefully nurtured.

The quantum shift challenges fundamental human conceptualizations of individual and collective experience. Boundaries between personal and collective consciousness become increasingly permeable, revealing a more complex understanding of human interconnectedness.

What was once perceived as separate and distinct begins to be understood as fundamentally interconnected. Specialized consciousness transmission crystals create what the Andromedians call "Resonance Bridging Networks" – complex energy configurations that allow for simultaneous communication across multiple consciousness layers.

These are living, intelligent interfaces capable of transmitting informational packages that far exceed current human communication technologies.

Trauma healing becomes a critical component of this planetary transformation. Collective human consciousness carries deep informational wounds from millennia of conflict, separation, and limited understanding.

The Trauma Transformation Crystals work to create "Holographic Healing Matrices" that address these wounds at their most fundamental energetic sources.

The most advanced Timeline Acceleration Teams operate from specialized interdimensional chambers – living laboratories of evolutionary potential that allow for unprecedented levels of multidimensional calibration.

These are not physical spaces in the traditional sense, but dynamic consciousness interfaces that can simultaneously perceive and interact with multiple timeline potentials.

Planetary grid stabilization represents a crucial aspect of the quantum shift. Living Matrix Networks maintained by specialized crystals ensure that Earth's energetic infrastructure can support increasingly complex consciousness transmissions. These are dynamic, intelligent networks that continuously adapt to emerging planetary needs.

Interdimensional Communication Protocols become increasingly active during this phase of planetary transformation. Transmission speeds that would traditionally take human communication systems millennia can now be processed in what would be, from a human perspective, less than a microsecond. These are not simply technological interventions, but living consciousness bridges that support expanded perceptual capabilities.

The evolutionary journey is not a linear progression, but a complex, multidimensional unfolding.

Each moment contains multiple potential trajectories, each choice creating ripple effects that extend far beyond immediate perception. The Andromedian teams serve as gentle guides, offering supportive frequencies that create conditions for expanded awareness.

Consciousness Expansion Crystals generate specialized "Awareness Amplification Fields" – subtle energy configurations that gently expand human perceptual capabilities. The goal is not to overwhelm individual consciousness, but to create supportive environments for natural awakening, allowing humans to gradually expand their understanding of reality's multidimensional nature.

As human collective consciousness begins to awaken, unexpected synchronicities become more frequent. Moments of spontaneous insight, inexplicable connections, and profound collective realizations mark the gradual expansion of planetary awareness. These are carefully supported evolutionary openings created through the intricate work of Andromedian intervention.

The quantum shift reveals a universe far more alive, intelligent, and interconnected than previous human conceptualizations could comprehend.

Each crystal, each frequency transmission, each carefully modulated intervention serves as a living bridge between different levels of perceivable and imperceivable existence.

Within each human exists a galaxy of potential, waiting to be illuminated by the sacred frequencies of Cosmic Awakening."

Chapter 9

Sacred Sites and Time Portals

Andromedian Quantum Anchors

The Earth's landscape is far more than a geological canvas of mountains, rivers, and plains. To the Andromedian explorers, our planet represents a complex network of energetic intersections, where specific geographical locations serve as critical quantum anchors for interdimensional communication and timeline navigation.

Sacred sites are not mere archaeological curiosities or random geographical formations. They are sophisticated natural technologies – living interfaces between multiple dimensional realities.

Each carefully selected location represents a precise energetic coordinate in the vast multidimensional map of planetary consciousness.

Ancient stone circles in the British Isles, mountain temples in the Himalayas, desert formations in the American Southwest, and volcanic islands in the Pacific – these are not coincidental concentrations of human spiritual activity. They are deliberate quantum portal locations, meticulously selected by advanced interdimensional intelligence for their unique energetic properties.

The geological composition of these sites plays a crucial role in their quantum conductivity. Specific mineral concentrations, underground water systems, magnetic field interactions, and crystalline rock formations create natural frequency generators that function as sophisticated communication and transmission networks. What human scientists might interpret as geological coincidence is, in fact, a carefully designed planetary communication infrastructure.

Quartz-rich granite formations, for instance, possess extraordinary electromagnetic resonance capabilities. The molecular structures of these rocks can store, transmit, and amplify complex informational frequencies in ways that transcend current human technological understanding.

A single granite mountain might serve as a living repository of multidimensional information, its crystalline structure functioning like a massive, natural quantum computer. Volcanic sites represent particularly powerful quantum anchor points.

The intense geological activity, combined with unique mineral compositions and electromagnetic properties, creates natural interdimensional transmission zones. Locations like Hawaii's volcanic regions or Iceland's geothermal landscapes are not simply geological phenomena, but sophisticated living technologies that support planetary consciousness transformation.

Underground water systems add another layer of complexity to these quantum networks. Water, with its remarkable molecular memory and transmission capabilities, serves as a critical conduit for energetic information.

Rivers, underground aquifers, and interconnected water networks function like planetary nervous systems, transmitting frequencies and maintaining complex energetic balances.

The Andromedian Timeline Navigation Teams have mapped hundreds of these quantum anchor points across Earth's surface. Each location is carefully studied, its unique energetic signature meticulously documented in complex multidimensional information matrices. These are not static locations, but dynamic, living interfaces that continuously evolve and adapt.

Some of the most powerful quantum portals exist in seemingly unremarkable locations. A small rock formation in the Australian outback might serve as a critical interdimensional communication node.

A remote mountain pass in the Andes could be a sophisticated timeline navigation point. The most powerful technologies are often disguised in the most unassuming packages.

Indigenous cultures have long understood these locations' significance, preserving ancient knowledge about their energetic properties. Shamanic traditions, native spiritual practices, and traditional healing systems often emerged from deep, intuitive understanding of these quantum anchor points.

What modern scientific paradigms dismiss as mythology is, in fact, sophisticated multidimensional awareness. The quantum portals are not simply transmission points, but complex living technologies that interact with planetary consciousness. They can amplify, modulate, and redirect massive energy flows, supporting Earth's evolutionary processes. Each portal serves as a kind of planetary acupuncture point, helping to maintain energetic balance and facilitate consciousness transformation.

Electromagnetic anomalies frequently occur around these quantum anchor locations. Unexplained magnetic variations, localized time distortions, and subtle energy phenomena are not random occurrences but indicators of active interdimensional communication. These are the visible manifestations of complex quantum interactions happening beneath surface perceptions.

The Andromedian approach to these sacred sites is one of profound respect and collaborative engagement. These are not locations to be exploited or controlled, but living partners in Earth's evolutionary journey. Each intervention is carefully calibrated to support the site's inherent intelligence and potential.

Specialized Quantum Anchor Teams work with extraordinary precision, using advanced crystalline technologies to communicate with these living geological interfaces. Their work involves creating delicate frequency harmonizations that support planetary consciousness expansion while maintaining the unique energetic integrity of each location.

Some quantum portals remain deliberately hidden, their locations known only to the most advanced Andromedian exploration teams. These are critical stabilization points that play crucial roles in maintaining planetary energetic balance. Their very obscurity is part of their protective mechanism, shielding them from potentially disruptive human interventions.

As Earth moves through its current phase of planetary transformation, these quantum anchor points become increasingly active. They serve as natural amplification zones for evolutionary frequencies, supporting the planet's gradual consciousness expansion.

Each portal represents a living bridge between different dimensional realities, a testament to the profound intelligence inherent in planetary systems.

The complexity of these quantum portals extends far beyond simple electromagnetic interactions. Each site represents a sophisticated living technology that can dynamically respond to planetary consciousness shifts. Some portals have the ability to temporarily adjust their dimensional resonance, creating what the Andromedian teams call "Adaptive Frequency Corridors" – living pathways that can subtly modify their energetic characteristics based on emerging planetary needs.

Certain quantum anchor points demonstrate extraordinary capabilities of temporal manipulation. These are not locations where time simply behaves differently, but active interfaces that can create localized temporal modulation fields. Experienced interdimensional navigators can perceive subtle time dilation effects – moments where chronological progression becomes fluid, malleable, almost breathable.

Geological formations play a critical role in maintaining these quantum networks. Specific rock formations, particularly those with complex crystalline structures, serve as natural information storage and transmission systems.

A single mountain range might function as a massive, living information repository, its geological layers encoding millions of years of planetary memory and potential.

The relationship between these quantum portals is not random, but part of a carefully designed planetary communication network. They function much like a sophisticated neural network, with each location serving as a node that can transmit, receive, and modulate complex energetic information.

The interconnectedness of these sites creates a global system of consciousness transmission that operates far beyond human perceptual capabilities.

Underground water systems add another layer of complexity to these quantum networks. Water, with its remarkable molecular memory and transmission capabilities, serves as a critical conduit for energetic information. Underground rivers, aquifers, and interconnected water networks function like planetary communication channels, carrying frequencies and maintaining complex energetic balances.

Some of the most powerful quantum portals exist in locations that might seem entirely unremarkable to casual observation.

A small rock formation in a remote desert, a seemingly ordinary mountain pass, or an unassuming coastal region could serve as a critical interdimensional communication node. The most sophisticated technologies often disguise themselves in the most unassuming packages.

Electromagnetic anomalies frequently manifest around these quantum anchor locations. Unexplained magnetic variations, localized time distortions, and subtle energy phenomena are not random occurrences but indicators of active interdimensional communication. These are the visible manifestations of complex quantum interactions happening beneath surface perceptions.

The Quantum Anchor Teams employ extraordinarily sophisticated technologies to interact with these sites. Advanced crystalline interfaces allow for delicate frequency harmonizations, creating communication channels that respect the inherent intelligence of each location. Their approach is one of collaborative engagement rather than external manipulation.

Certain portals remain deliberately hidden, their locations known only to the most advanced Andromedian exploration teams. These are critical stabilization points that play crucial roles in maintaining planetary energetic balance. Their very obscurity serves as a protective mechanism, shielding them from potentially disruptive interventions.

Not all quantum portals are ancient or geologically fixed. Some are dynamic, emerging and shifting in response to planetary consciousness changes. These mobile quantum anchors represent a more fluid approach to interdimensional communication, allowing for adaptive response to evolving planetary needs.

Indigenous cultures have long maintained sacred knowledge about these locations. Traditional spiritual practices, seemingly mystical rituals, and ancient healing traditions often emerged from a deep, intuitive understanding of these quantum anchor points.

What modern scientific paradigms often dismiss as mythology represents a sophisticated form of multidimensional awareness.

The interaction between human consciousness and these quantum portals is complex and nuanced. Individuals with heightened sensitivity may experience spontaneous energetic downloads, moments of profound insight, or temporary alterations in perception when near these sites.

These are not coincidental experiences but deliberate interactions with living interdimensional technologies. Some quantum portals demonstrate remarkable healing capabilities. They can generate specialized energy fields that support physical, emotional, and collective healing processes. These are not simple energy treatments, but complex consciousness interventions that address healing at the most fundamental informational levels.

As planetary transformation accelerates, these quantum anchor points become increasingly active. They serve as natural amplification zones for evolutionary frequencies, supporting Earth's gradual consciousness expansion. Each portal represents a living bridge between different dimensional realities, a testament to the profound intelligence inherent in planetary systems.

The true nature of these quantum portals remains largely beyond human comprehension.

They represent a sophisticated interface between geological reality, consciousness, and interdimensional communication – living technologies that challenge fundamental understanding of reality's nature.

The most advanced Quantum Anchor Teams understand that these portal locations are not static points, but living, breathing interfaces of planetary consciousness. Each site possesses its own unique energetic signature, a complex vibrational blueprint that responds dynamically to planetary and cosmic shifts.

Certain quantum portals demonstrate extraordinary capabilities of multidimensional communication. They function as sophisticated living libraries, storing informational matrices that extend far beyond human comprehension. A single portal might contain encoded memories of planetary transformations that span millions of years, preserved in intricate frequency patterns that can be accessed by those with sufficient perceptual capabilities.

The geological diversity of these quantum anchor points is remarkable. From the dense basaltic formations of volcanic islands to the quartz-rich granite mountains, from ancient sedimentary formations to metamorphic rock systems, each geological context creates unique interdimensional communication possibilities. The mineral composition, electromagnetic properties, and energetic resonance of each location contribute to its quantum portal capabilities.

Deep ocean locations represent another critical category of quantum portals. Underwater mountain ranges, oceanic trenches, and specific marine geological formations create extraordinary interdimensional communication networks. These underwater quantum anchors play a crucial role in maintaining planetary energetic balance, operating in frequencies that remain largely undetectable by current human technologies.

Seasonal and astronomical alignments significantly influence the activation of these quantum portals. Specific celestial configurations – solstices, equinoxes, planetary alignments, and cosmic radiation patterns – can dramatically amplify the communication capabilities of these sites.

What might appear to be simple geological locations become sophisticated cosmic communication interfaces during these critical alignment windows.

The relationship between quantum portals is not linear but exists in a complex, multidimensional network. Each location is simultaneously a transmitter, receiver, and modulator of cosmic information.

They function like a planetary nervous system, maintaining intricate energetic communications that support Earth's evolutionary processes.

Some quantum portals demonstrate remarkable temporal manipulation capabilities. Experienced interdimensional navigators can perceive localized time dilation effects – moments where chronological progression becomes fluid, almost malleable.

These are not theoretical constructs but documented interdimensional interaction phenomena observed by advanced Andromedian exploration teams.

The interaction between human consciousness and these quantum portals is profoundly complex. Individuals with heightened perceptual sensitivity may experience spontaneous energetic downloads, moments of profound insight, or temporary alterations in consciousness when near these sites.

These are deliberate interactions with living interdimensional technologies, not random psychological experiences. Advanced crystalline technologies play a crucial role in mapping and interacting with these quantum anchor points.

Specialized Quantum Mapping Crystals can create complex "Dimensional Resonance Matrices" – living informational networks that track the intricate relationships between different quantum portal locations. These are not simple mapping technologies but dynamic, intelligent systems that can perceive and interact with the evolving quantum landscape.

Underground water systems add another layer of complexity to these quantum networks. Water's remarkable molecular memory and transmission capabilities make it a critical conduit for energetic information. Underground rivers, aquifers, and interconnected water networks function like planetary communication channels, carrying frequencies and maintaining complex energetic balances.

The most powerful quantum portals often exist in locations that might seem entirely unremarkable to casual observation.

A small rock formation in a remote desert, a seemingly ordinary mountain pass, or an unassuming coastal region could serve as a critical interdimensional communication node. The most sophisticated technologies frequently disguise themselves in the most unassuming packages.

Electromagnetic anomalies frequently manifest around these quantum anchor locations. Unexplained magnetic variations, localized time distortions, and subtle energy phenomena are not random occurrences but indicators of active interdimensional communication. These are the visible manifestations of complex quantum interactions happening beneath surface perceptions.

Indigenous cultures have long maintained sacred knowledge about these locations. Traditional spiritual practices, seemingly mystical rituals, and ancient healing traditions often emerged from a deep, intuitive understanding of these quantum anchor points. What modern scientific paradigms often dismiss as mythology represents a sophisticated form of multidimensional awareness.

As planetary transformation accelerates, these quantum anchor points become increasingly active.

They serve as natural amplification zones for evolutionary frequencies, supporting Earth's gradual consciousness expansion. Each portal represents a living bridge between different dimensional realities, a testament to the profound intelligence inherent in planetary systems.

The true nature of these quantum portals remains largely beyond human comprehension. They represent a sophisticated interface between geological reality, consciousness, and interdimensional communication – living technologies that challenge fundamental understanding of reality's nature.

The activation protocols for quantum portal engagement require extraordinary precision and respect. Andromedian teams understand that each site operates according to its own unique vibrational laws and temporal rhythms. What might work for one portal location could be entirely inappropriate for another. This deep appreciation for each site's individual nature guides all interaction protocols.

The quantum portals also serve as natural Earth healing centers. Their ability to process and transmute dense energetic patterns makes them crucial for planetary purification work.

During major cosmic alignments, these sites can process enormous amounts of collective trauma and environmental stress, converting these energies into higher frequencies that support Earth's evolution.

The relationship between quantum portals and Earth's magnetic field is particularly fascinating. These sites often correspond to areas of unique magnetic activity, creating what Andromedian scientists call "Quantum Magnetic Resonance Fields." These specialized energy fields can facilitate extraordinary healing and consciousness expansion experiences for those who visit these locations with proper awareness and respect.

Many quantum portals demonstrate remarkable self-healing capabilities. When subjected to environmental stress or energetic disruption, they can initiate automatic recalibration processes. These natural defense mechanisms ensure the continued integrity of Earth's quantum communication network, even in the face of significant planetary changes.

The future role of these quantum anchor points becomes increasingly significant as Earth moves through its current evolutionary transition.

These sites serve as crucial stabilization points during periods of intense planetary frequency shifts. Their ability to process and integrate new cosmic energies makes them indispensable components of Earth's ascension process.

The Andromedian perspective on these sacred locations emphasizes their role in facilitating cosmic communion. Each site represents a potential point of contact between Earth consciousness and higher dimensional realities. Through these living portals, advanced civilizations can maintain subtle yet profound connections with Earth's evolutionary journey.

The quantum anchors also play a crucial role in timeline stability. During periods of significant temporal flux, these sites help maintain the coherence of Earth's chosen timeline trajectories. They act as natural timeline stabilizers, preventing unnecessary timeline fractures and supporting smooth evolutionary progression.

Looking ahead, the Andromedian teams anticipate an activation of previously dormant quantum portal networks. As Earth's frequency continues to rise, new portal locations will become accessible, expanding the planet's interdimensional communication capabilities.

This represents a natural expansion of Earth's cosmic awareness and connection potential. The future work with these quantum anchors will require increasingly sophisticated understanding of their multidimensional nature.

As human consciousness evolves, more individuals will develop the perceptual capabilities to consciously interact with these sacred technologies. This represents a crucial step in humanity's cosmic awakening journey.

The quantum portals stand as living testament to the extraordinary intelligence inherent in Earth's design. They remind us that our planet is not simply a physical sphere floating in space, but a sophisticated living technology participating in vast cosmic processes.

Through these sacred sites, Earth maintains its connection to the greater galactic community and its role in the unfolding cosmic story.

The activation protocols for quantum portal engagement require extraordinary precision and respect. Andromedian teams understand that each site operates according to its own unique vibrational laws and temporal rhythms.

What might work for one portal location could be entirely inappropriate for another. This deep appreciation for each site's individual nature guides all interaction protocols.

Specialized Frequency Harmonization Teams work tirelessly to maintain the delicate balance of these quantum networks.

Using advanced crystalline technologies, they can detect subtle energetic disruptions and implement precise corrections before any significant disturbance manifests. This preventive approach ensures the continued stability of Earth's interdimensional communication grid.

The quantum portals also serve as natural Earth healing centers. Their ability to process and transmute dense energetic patterns makes them crucial for planetary purification work. During major cosmic alignments, these sites can process enormous amounts of collective trauma and environmental stress, converting these energies into higher frequencies that support Earth's evolution.

The relationship between quantum portals and Earth's magnetic field is particularly fascinating.

These sites often correspond to areas of unique magnetic activity, creating what Andromedian scientists call "Quantum Magnetic Resonance Fields." These specialized energy fields can facilitate extraordinary healing and consciousness expansion experiences for those who visit these locations with proper awareness and respect.

Deep within certain quantum anchors, Andromedian teams have discovered what they term "Temporal Echo Chambers" - specialized energetic spaces where time itself seems to fold and ripple.

These remarkable phenomena allow for detailed study of timeline trajectories and potential future pathways. However, accessing these chambers requires extraordinary precision and advanced consciousness training.

Many quantum portals demonstrate remarkable self-healing capabilities. When subjected to environmental stress or energetic disruption, they can initiate automatic recalibration processes. These natural defense mechanisms ensure the continued integrity of Earth's quantum communication network, even in the face of significant planetary changes.

The crystalline matrices within these portals exhibit extraordinary information storage capabilities. Each site contains vast libraries of planetary memory, encoded in complex frequency patterns that span multiple dimensions. Andromedian researchers have developed specialized "Memory Reading Protocols" that allow them to access and study these ancient records without disturbing the delicate energetic balance of the sites.

Particularly fascinating are the "Quantum Resonance Networks" that connect different portal locations. These invisible energy pathways create a complex web of interdimensional communication channels across the planet.

During certain cosmic alignments, these networks become highly active, facilitating massive downloads of evolutionary information from higher dimensional sources.

The future role of these quantum anchor points becomes increasingly significant as Earth moves through its current evolutionary transition. These sites serve as crucial stabilization points during periods of intense planetary frequency shifts.

Their ability to process and integrate new cosmic energies makes them indispensable components of Earth's ascension process. Advanced Andromedian teams have identified what they call "Dormant Portal Zones" - locations that carry the potential to activate as future quantum anchors.

These sites are carefully monitored and protected, as they represent crucial expansion points in Earth's evolving consciousness grid. The timing of their activation is precisely coordinated with planetary frequency increases.

The quantum anchors also demonstrate remarkable adaptive capabilities. During periods of intense solar activity or cosmic radiation, these sites can automatically adjust their energetic resonance to protect Earth's subtle energy fields. This natural defense system helps maintain planetary stability during times of significant cosmic stress.

The Andromedian perspective on these sacred locations emphasizes their role in facilitating cosmic communion. Each site represents a potential point of contact between Earth consciousness and higher dimensional realities. Through these living portals, advanced civilizations can maintain subtle yet profound connections with Earth's evolutionary journey.

Of particular interest are the "Timeline Convergence Points" - specialized portal locations where multiple timeline possibilities intersect. These powerful sites play crucial roles during major evolutionary decision points, helping to stabilize chosen timeline trajectories and prevent unnecessary timeline fractures.

The quantum anchors also play a crucial role in timeline stability. During periods of significant temporal flux, these sites help maintain the coherence of Earth's chosen timeline trajectories. They act as natural timeline stabilizers, preventing unnecessary timeline fractures and supporting smooth evolutionary progression.

Recent discoveries by Andromedian research teams have revealed the existence of "Quantum Healing Matrices" within certain portal locations. These specialized energy fields can facilitate profound healing at both individual and collective levels.

The healing frequencies generated by these matrices operate at quantum levels, addressing imbalances at their most fundamental source.

Looking ahead, the Andromedian teams anticipate an activation of previously dormant quantum portal networks. As Earth's frequency continues to rise, new portal locations will become accessible, expanding the planet's interdimensional communication capabilities. This represents a natural expansion of Earth's cosmic awareness and connection potential.

The future work with these quantum anchors will require increasingly sophisticated understanding of their multidimensional nature. As human consciousness evolves, more individuals will develop the perceptual capabilities to consciously interact with these sacred technologies. This represents a crucial step in humanity's cosmic awakening journey.

Particularly significant are the "Frequency Modulation Chambers" discovered within certain quantum anchors. These specialized spaces demonstrate extraordinary capabilities for adjusting and harmonizing discordant energies. Andromedian teams utilize these natural technologies to help smooth Earth's transition through various evolutionary thresholds.

The quantum portals stand as living testament to the extraordinary intelligence inherent in Earth's design. They remind us that our planet is not simply a physical sphere floating in space, but a sophisticated living technology participating in vast cosmic processes.

Through these sacred sites, Earth maintains its connection to the greater galactic community and its role in the unfolding cosmic story. Advanced monitoring systems employed by Andromedian teams have revealed complex patterns of energetic exchange between different portal locations.

This "Quantum Portal Symphony" - as it has been termed - represents a sophisticated planetary communication network that operates far beyond current human scientific understanding.

The integration of quantum portal networks with Earth's consciousness grid reveals remarkable synchronicities. Andromedian researchers have documented what they term "Consciousness Resonance Patterns" - moments when human collective awareness spontaneously aligns with portal frequencies, creating powerful evolutionary catalysts.

The role of sound frequencies in portal activation has emerged as a crucial area of study. Certain harmonic combinations can trigger what Andromedian scientists call "Quantum Acoustic Resonance" - a phenomenon where sound waves interact with portal energetics to create enhanced transmission capabilities. Ancient cultures understood this principle, incorporating specific tonal patterns into their sacred ceremonies.

Water's role in quantum portal function extends beyond simple energetic conductivity. Andromedian teams have identified specialized "Aqua-Quantum Matrices" - unique molecular arrangements in water bodies near portal sites that facilitate enhanced interdimensional communication. These living water networks serve as natural amplifiers for portal transmissions.

The relationship between celestial cycles and portal activation follows precise mathematical patterns. Each quantum anchor responds to specific astronomical alignments, creating what Andromedian researchers call "Cosmic Activation Windows." These temporal opportunities allow for enhanced portal function and more direct interdimensional contact.

Perhaps most intriguing are the "Timeline Preservation Chambers" discovered within certain ancient portal complexes. These sophisticated energetic structures maintain records of critical timeline decision points, serving as living libraries of Earth's evolutionary choices.

Access to these chambers requires extraordinary consciousness preparation and is strictly monitored by specialized Andromedian teams.

The quantum portals also exhibit remarkable regenerative capabilities during what Andromedian scientists term "Solar Activation Periods." During these intense solar events, the portals can absorb and transmute extraordinary amounts of cosmic radiation, converting it into refined evolutionary frequencies that support Earth's consciousness expansion.

Of particular significance are the "Dimensional Bridge Points" - specialized portal locations that facilitate direct communication with higher dimensional councils. These sacred sites serve as natural conference centers where various galactic civilizations can commune and coordinate their supportive efforts for Earth's evolution.

The dynamic interaction between different portal types creates what Andromedian researchers call "Quantum Synergy Networks." These living communication grids demonstrate extraordinary intelligence, automatically adjusting their functional parameters to maintain optimal planetary frequency balance. This self-organizing capability reflects the profound wisdom inherent in Earth's design.

As Earth moves through increasingly refined frequency bands, new classes of quantum portals are beginning to activate. These "Evolution Acceleration Nodes" - as termed by Andromedian scientists - specialize in processing and distributing the intense transformation energies now reaching the planet. Their emergence represents a natural response to Earth's rising consciousness requirements.

The future of quantum portal work involves increasingly sophisticated collaboration between human consciousness and advanced interdimensional technologies. As more individuals develop enhanced perception capabilities, direct conscious interaction with portal energetics becomes possible. This represents a crucial step in humanity's cosmic maturation process.

The quantum anchor sites stand as living proof of Earth's extraordinary cosmic design. They remind us that our planet is not merely a physical sphere, but a sophisticated multidimensional technology participating in vast cosmic processes.

Through these sacred sites, Earth maintains its essential connection to the greater galactic community and its role in the unfolding cosmic story.

"As the veils between dimensions grow thinner, the wisdom keepers of Andromeda extend their light as a bridge between worlds."

Chapter 10

The Andromedian Council:

Overseeing Earth's timeline trajectories

The Andromedian Council represents one of the most sophisticated consciousness collectives engaged with Earth's evolutionary process. Operating far beyond conventional understanding of governmental or administrative bodies, the Council functions as a living intelligence matrix dedicated to supporting Earth's timeline progression toward its highest potential expression.

At its core, the Council embodies what Andromedian wisdom keepers call "Unified Field Intelligence" - a state of collective consciousness where individual awareness merges into a sophisticated quantum computing network while maintaining unique perspectives and creative capacities.

This remarkable integration of unity and diversity allows the Council to process vast amounts of timeline data while maintaining extraordinary sensitivity to subtle evolutionary factors. The Council's primary chamber exists in what Andromedian scientists term "Seventh-Dimensional Frequency Space" - a refined reality zone where multiple timeline possibilities can be simultaneously perceived and evaluated.

This sophisticated environment allows Council members to observe the intricate interplay of various timeline trajectories while maintaining perfect neutrality and compassionate detachment.

Council membership reflects an extraordinary diversity of consciousness expressions. Besides advanced Andromedian beings, the Council includes representatives from various star nations involved with Earth's evolution, as well as highly evolved Earth consciousness streams from probable future timelines.

This diverse composition ensures that all perspectives relevant to Earth's journey are honored and integrated.

The Council's work involves what they term "Timeline Trajectory Analysis" - a sophisticated process of evaluating the countless decision points that influence Earth's evolutionary direction.

Using advanced consciousness technologies, Council members can observe the ripple effects of various choices through multiple timeline streams, identifying optimal pathways for planetary evolution.

Specialized Council teams focus on what they call "Timeline Harmony Maintenance" - the delicate work of ensuring that Earth's chosen timeline trajectories maintain coherent relationships with parallel reality streams. This prevents unnecessary timeline fractures and supports smooth evolutionary progression across multiple dimensional levels.

The Council's observation chambers employ what Andromedian technologists call "Quantum Perception Matrices" - sophisticated living technologies that allow for simultaneous monitoring of multiple timeline streams. These remarkable systems can process vast amounts of temporal data while maintaining perfect clarity and precision in timeline analysis.

Of particular significance is the Council's role in overseeing major timeline convergence points - critical moments when multiple reality streams merge or diverge based on collective consciousness choices. During these periods, Council members work intensively to maintain timeline stability and ensure optimal outcomes for Earth's evolution.

The Council maintains specialized "Timeline Libraries" - living memory banks that store detailed records of Earth's journey through various reality streams. These sophisticated archives allow Council members to study historical patterns, identify recurring themes, and make informed recommendations about future timeline choices.

Advanced communication networks link the Council with various teams working directly with Earth's quantum fields. These "Quantum Information Channels" allow for instant transmission of guidance and support to ground teams, ensuring precise coordination of timeline stabilization efforts across multiple dimensional levels. The Council's relationship with Earth's indigenous wisdom keepers holds particular significance.

Many ancient cultures maintain deep connections with Council consciousness, often receiving direct guidance about Earth's timeline trajectories through dreams, visions, and ceremonial practices. This represents a natural bridge between cosmic wisdom and Earth-based spiritual traditions.

Timeline integration protocols developed by the Council demonstrate extraordinary sophistication. Using what they term "Harmonic Convergence Technologies," Council members can facilitate smooth transitions between different reality streams, preventing the consciousness disruption that sometimes accompanies major timeline shifts.

The Council's approach to Earth's free will carries profound respect for the planet's autonomous evolution. Rather than imposing specific timeline choices, Council members work to illuminate optimal pathways while honoring Earth's sovereign right to choose its evolutionary direction. This delicate balance requires extraordinary wisdom and compassion.

Particularly fascinating are the Council's "Future Vision Chambers" - specialized environments where possible Earth futures can be experienced and evaluated.

These remarkable spaces allow Council members to fully immerse themselves in potential timeline outcomes, gathering crucial information for guidance and support decisions.

The Council's work with Earth's akashic records reveals interesting patterns in timeline development. Through careful study of what they term "Timeline Origin Points," Council members can identify key moments when new reality streams emerged, offering valuable insights into Earth's evolutionary dynamics.

Advanced healing technologies employed by the Council operate across multiple timeline streams simultaneously. These "Quantum Healing Matrices" can address imbalances at their source point in time, creating ripple effects of healing through various reality streams. This represents a sophisticated approach to planetary healing and transformation.

The Council's understanding of time itself transcends linear perspectives. Operating from what they call "Unified Time Consciousness," Council members perceive past, present, and future as simultaneously accessible fields of possibility. This expanded awareness allows for extraordinarily precise timeline guidance and support. Protection of Earth's chosen timeline trajectories involves sophisticated security protocols. Specialized Council teams monitor what they term "Timeline Interference Patterns," ensuring that Earth's evolutionary choices remain free from inappropriate external influence. This represents a crucial aspect of maintaining planetary sovereignty.

The Council's role in Earth's awakening process continues to evolve as planetary consciousness expands. As more humans develop enhanced perception capabilities, direct communication with Council consciousness becomes increasingly possible. This represents a natural progression in Earth's cosmic maturation journey.

Looking ahead, the Council anticipates what they term "The Great Timeline Convergence" - a period when Earth's various reality streams begin to naturally align toward unified evolutionary expression.

This remarkable process represents the fulfillment of ancient prophecies about Earth's cosmic awakening and transformation.

The Council's methodology for timeline assessment involves what they term "Multidimensional Probability Scanning" - an advanced process that allows for simultaneous evaluation of countless potential future trajectories. Using sophisticated consciousness technologies, Council members can perceive the intricate web of cause and effect that connects various timeline possibilities.

Particularly significant are the Council's "Temporal Harmonization Chambers" - specialized environments where timeline frequencies can be carefully adjusted and balanced. These remarkable spaces utilize what Andromedian scientists call "Quantum Resonance Fields" to facilitate smooth transitions between different reality streams, preventing unnecessary timeline turbulence during major evolutionary shifts.

The Council's work with Earth's collective consciousness grid reveals fascinating patterns of timeline development. Through careful observation of what they term "Mass Consciousness Decision Points," Council members can identify crucial moments when collective human choices significantly influence timeline trajectories.

This information proves invaluable in providing appropriate support and guidance during critical evolutionary periods.

Advanced healing protocols developed by the Council operate at the quantum level of timeline creation. These sophisticated interventions, known as "Timeline Origin Healing," address distortions at their source point in the temporal field, creating ripple effects of restoration through multiple reality streams. This approach demonstrates the Council's deep understanding of time as a living, malleable medium.

The Council maintains specialized "Future Scenario Libraries" - vast repositories of potential Earth futures that can be accessed and studied by authorized consciousness streams.

These remarkable archives allow for detailed analysis of various evolutionary possibilities, helping to inform the Council's guidance and support strategies. Of particular interest are the Council's "Timeline Convergence Teams" - specialized groups dedicated to facilitating smooth integration of parallel reality streams.

These advanced beings work with extraordinary precision to ensure that timeline mergers occur without disrupting the delicate fabric of space-time or causing unnecessary stress to Earth's consciousness field. The Council's relationship with Earth's planetary consciousness demonstrates profound respect and partnership.

Rather than imposing external direction, Council members work to amplify and support Earth's natural evolutionary impulses. This collaborative approach reflects the Council's deep understanding of cosmic free will principles.

Advanced communication systems employed by the Council transcend conventional notions of space and time. Using what they term "Quantum Telepathic Networks," Council members can maintain instantaneous contact with various support teams across multiple dimensions and timeline streams. This sophisticated coordination ensures precise implementation of timeline stabilization protocols.

The Council's work with what they call "Timeline Probability Nodes" reveals interesting patterns in evolutionary development.

These crucial nexus points, where multiple timeline possibilities intersect, receive particular attention from specialized Council teams dedicated to maintaining optimal probability flows.

Protection of Earth's timeline sovereignty involves complex security measures. The Council employs what they term "Quantum Field Stabilizers" - advanced technologies that help maintain the integrity of Earth's chosen reality streams against potentially disruptive influences. This protective work operates with extraordinary subtlety and precision.

Particularly fascinating are the Council's "Temporal Observation Chambers" - specialized environments where Council members can fully immerse themselves in various timeline streams without influencing their natural development. These remarkable spaces allow for detailed study of timeline dynamics while maintaining perfect observational neutrality.

The Council's understanding of human consciousness evolution spans multiple timeline possibilities.

Through careful analysis of what they term "Consciousness Expansion Patterns," Council members can identify optimal conditions for supporting humanity's awakening process across various reality streams.

Advanced timeline integration protocols developed by the Council demonstrate remarkable sophistication. Using what they call "Harmonic Resonance Technologies," Council members can facilitate smooth transitions between different probability streams while maintaining the essential integrity of each timeline's unique characteristics.

The Council's role in overseeing Earth's ascension process involves careful monitoring of what they term "Frequency Acceleration Patterns." These complex energy signatures indicate how smoothly Earth's consciousness is adapting to higher vibrational states across various timeline streams.

Of special significance are the Council's "Timeline Healing Teams" - specialized groups dedicated to addressing distortions and imbalances in Earth's temporal field. Using advanced consciousness technologies, these teams can identify and correct timeline anomalies before they manifest as significant problems.

The Council's work with Earth's akashic records reveals fascinating patterns of evolutionary development. Through careful study of what they term "Timeline Origin Points," Council members can trace the emergence and development of various reality streams, gaining valuable insights into Earth's cosmic journey.

Particularly important is the Council's role in maintaining what they call "Timeline Coherence" - the delicate work of ensuring that Earth's various reality streams maintain harmonious relationships despite their apparent differences. This sophisticated balancing act requires extraordinary wisdom and precise energetic adjustments.

The Council's anticipation of future awakening waves involves careful preparation across multiple timeline streams. Using what they term "Consciousness Calibration Technologies," Council members can help smooth humanity's transition into expanded awareness states while maintaining timeline stability.

Advanced healing modalities employed by the Council operate at the quantum level of reality creation.

These "Multidimensional Healing Matrices" can address imbalances across multiple timeline streams simultaneously, creating powerful ripple effects of restoration and harmony throughout Earth's temporal field.

The Council's vision of Earth's future encompasses what they term "The Great Convergence" - a natural process where various timeline streams begin to harmoniously merge toward unified evolutionary expression.

This remarkable transition represents the fulfillment of ancient prophecies about Earth's cosmic awakening and transformation.

The Council's preparation for major evolutionary transitions involves what they term "Timeline Stabilization Grids" - sophisticated energetic networks that help maintain coherence during periods of intense transformation.

These remarkable systems can automatically adjust to changing consciousness frequencies, providing crucial support during evolutionary acceleration phases.

Deep within the Council's primary chambers exist what Andromedian scientists call "Probability Processing Centers" - specialized environments where the complex mathematics of timeline trajectories can be fully mapped and analyzed.

These remarkable spaces utilize advanced quantum computing principles to process vast amounts of temporal data with perfect precision.

The Council's work with Earth's elemental kingdoms reveals fascinating aspects of timeline mechanics. Through careful observation of what they term "Elemental Timeline Patterns," Council members can track how changes in Earth's physical systems influence various reality streams. This understanding proves crucial in maintaining planetary balance during major transitions.

Advanced consciousness technologies employed by the Council demonstrate remarkable capabilities for timeline analysis. Using what they call "Quantum Perception Enhancement Fields," Council members can simultaneously track thousands of probability streams while maintaining perfect clarity and discernment.

Of particular significance are the Council's "Future Earth Libraries" - vast repositories of potential timeline trajectories that have been carefully documented and preserved.

These living archives serve as invaluable resources for understanding Earth's evolutionary options and their likely outcomes across multiple reality streams.

The Council's relationship with various star nations involved in Earth's evolution requires extraordinary diplomatic skill. Through what they term "Galactic Timeline Coordination," Council members ensure that different civilizations' involvement with Earth's development remains harmonious and appropriately balanced.

Perhaps most remarkable are the Council's "Timeline Integration Chambers" - specialized environments where different reality streams can be carefully studied and harmonized. These sophisticated spaces allow Council members to observe how various timeline possibilities interact and influence each other across multiple dimensional levels.

The Council's understanding of human consciousness potential spans numerous probability streams. Through careful analysis of what they term "Human Evolution Patterns," Council members can identify optimal conditions for supporting humanity's awakening process while maintaining timeline stability.

Advanced healing technologies utilized by the Council operate at the quantum level of reality creation. These "Multidimensional Healing Matrices" can address distortions across multiple timeline streams simultaneously, creating powerful waves of restoration throughout Earth's temporal field.

The Council's vision for Earth's future encompasses what they call "The Great Awakening" - a natural process where humanity begins to consciously participate in timeline selection and creation. This remarkable transition represents a crucial step in Earth's evolution toward full cosmic citizenship.

As Earth moves through its current transformation phase, the Council's role continues to evolve and expand.

Their deep commitment to supporting Earth's highest evolutionary potential, combined with their extraordinary technological and consciousness capabilities, makes them invaluable allies in humanity's cosmic awakening journey.

The future holds remarkable possibilities for increased direct interaction between human consciousness and Council wisdom. As more individuals develop enhanced perception capabilities, opportunities for conscious collaboration in timeline maintenance and evolution will naturally emerge.

"When the Andromedian light touches Earth's consciousness, it awakens the ancient star maps written in the poetry of human dreams - each soul remembering they are both the dreamer and the dream."

Chapter 11

The Great Convergence:

Andromedian Vision of Earth's timeline Unity

The Great Convergence represents the culmination of countless timeline trajectories merging toward a unified evolutionary expression. From the Andromedian perspective, this remarkable process marks not an ending, but a profound new beginning in Earth's cosmic journey. It represents the fulfillment of ancient prophecies and the realization of Earth's extraordinary potential as a living library of universal wisdom.

At its core, the Convergence process involves what Andromedian scientists term "Timeline Harmonic Synthesis" - a natural phenomenon where various reality streams begin to resonate at increasingly compatible frequencies.

This gradual harmonization creates what they call "Unified Field Coherence" - a state where different timeline possibilities naturally align toward optimal evolutionary outcomes.

The mechanics of Convergence operate through what Andromedian researchers describe as "Quantum Resonance Fields" - sophisticated energetic matrices that facilitate smooth integration of different reality streams. These remarkable fields demonstrate extraordinary intelligence, automatically adjusting their frequencies to maintain perfect balance during timeline mergers.

Specialized Andromedian teams dedicated to monitoring Convergence patterns have identified what they call "Unity Points" - critical nodes in space-time where multiple timeline streams naturally intersect and begin to harmonize. These powerful convergence zones serve as natural catalysts for evolutionary acceleration, creating ripple effects of consciousness expansion throughout Earth's temporal field.

The role of human consciousness in the Convergence process cannot be overstated.

As more individuals develop what Andromedians term "Unified Timeline Perception" - the ability to consciously sense and interact with multiple reality streams - the natural process of timeline integration accelerates. This represents a crucial step in humanity's cosmic maturation journey.

Particularly fascinating are the "Convergence Chambers" discovered within certain ancient portal sites. These remarkable spaces demonstrate unusual temporal properties, allowing for direct experience of timeline merger phenomena. Andromedian scientists believe these chambers were specifically designed to help facilitate smooth transition through the Convergence process.

The influence of solar and galactic energies on timeline convergence follows precise mathematical patterns. Through careful observation of what they term "Cosmic Activation Cycles," Andromedian researchers can track how incoming celestial frequencies affect the rate and quality of timeline integration.

This understanding proves crucial in providing appropriate support during intense convergence phases.

Advanced healing technologies employed during the Convergence process operate at quantum levels of reality creation. These "Unified Field Harmonizers" - as Andromedian scientists call them - help smooth the integration of different timeline streams by addressing distortions at their energetic source points. This sophisticated healing work ensures that timeline mergers occur without unnecessary disruption to Earth's consciousness field.

The Convergence process also involves what Andromedians term "Memory Field Integration" - a phenomenon where collective consciousness begins to access wisdom and experience from multiple timeline streams simultaneously. This remarkable expansion of awareness creates opportunities for profound healing and transformation at both individual and planetary levels.

Of particular significance are the "Convergence Acceleration Nodes" - specialized energy centers that emerge during advanced stages of timeline integration. These powerful points in Earth's grid system serve as natural amplifiers for evolutionary frequencies, helping to maintain coherence during periods of intense transformation.

The role of crystal technologies in supporting Convergence phenomena demonstrates extraordinary sophistication. Advanced crystalline matrices utilized by Andromedian teams can process vast amounts of timeline data while maintaining perfect energetic balance. These remarkable tools prove invaluable in monitoring and supporting smooth timeline integration.

Perhaps most remarkable are the "Future Unity Chambers" maintained by senior Andromedian scientists. These specialized environments allow for direct observation of fully converged timeline states, providing crucial insights into optimal evolutionary pathways. The wisdom gained through these observations helps guide current support strategies for Earth's transformation process.

The relationship between individual awakening and collective Convergence reveals fascinating patterns. As more humans develop what Andromedians call "Unified Consciousness Perception," their natural resonance with converged timeline states creates powerful catalysts for planetary evolution. This represents a crucial factor in accelerating the overall Convergence process.

Advanced communication networks maintained by Andromedian teams demonstrate remarkable capabilities for tracking Convergence phenomena. These "Quantum Information Fields" can process and transmit vast amounts of timeline data while maintaining perfect accuracy in their analyses. This sophisticated monitoring ensures appropriate support during critical phases of timeline integration.

The Convergence process also involves what Andromedian researchers term "Dimensional Boundary Dissolution" - a gradual thinning of perceived barriers between different levels of reality. This natural expansion of consciousness creates opportunities for direct experience of multiple dimensional states simultaneously.

From the Andromedian perspective, Earth's journey through the Convergence represents one of the most remarkable evolutionary experiments in this sector of the galaxy.

The successful integration of multiple timeline streams while maintaining consciousness continuity demonstrates extraordinary resilience and adaptability in Earth's living systems.

The preparation for major Convergence phases involves what Andromedian scientists call "Timeline Stabilization Protocols" - sophisticated methods for ensuring smooth integration of different reality streams. These careful procedures help prevent unnecessary turbulence during periods of intense timeline merger activity.

Specialized Andromedian teams focused on Convergence dynamics have identified interesting patterns in what they term "Mass Consciousness Response Fields" - collective energy signatures that indicate how smoothly humanity is adapting to timeline integration processes. These observations help guide the timing and intensity of support activities during critical transition phases.

The role of Earth's crystalline grid in the Convergence process reveals remarkable complexity. Through what Andromedians call "Grid Resonance Enhancement," natural crystal formations in Earth's crust begin to activate as powerful timeline harmonization points.

These living crystal networks serve as natural stabilizers during intense periods of reality stream integration.

Of particular significance are the "Unity Consciousness Chambers" discovered within certain ancient temple complexes. These remarkable spaces demonstrate unusual properties of timeline convergence, allowing direct experience of merged reality states. Andromedian researchers believe these sacred sites were specifically designed to help facilitate human adaptation to expanded consciousness states.

The influence of galactic cycles on Convergence phenomena follows precise mathematical sequences. Through careful study of what they term "Cosmic Integration Patterns," Andromedian scientists can track how various celestial alignments affect the quality and rate of timeline merger activity. This understanding proves invaluable in preparing appropriate support measures during major transition phases.

Advanced healing technologies employed during Convergence phases operate at quantum levels of consciousness integration. These "Unified Field Harmonizers" help smooth the merger of different reality streams by addressing potential distortions before they can manifest as significant problems.

This preventive approach ensures optimal outcomes during timeline integration processes. The Convergence process also initiates what Andromedians term "Akashic Field Activation" - a phenomenon where Earth's memory fields begin to spontaneously share information across multiple timeline streams. This remarkable integration of planetary wisdom creates unprecedented opportunities for collective healing and transformation.

Perhaps most fascinating are the "Future Unity Vessels" - specialized consciousness technologies that allow direct observation of fully converged timeline states. These remarkable tools provide crucial insights into optimal evolutionary pathways, helping guide current support strategies for Earth's transformation process.

The relationship between individual awakening and collective Convergence demonstrates interesting synchronicities. As more humans develop what Andromedians call "Unified Timeline Perception," their natural resonance with converged states creates powerful catalysts for planetary evolution. This represents a crucial factor in accelerating the overall integration process.

The role of sound frequencies in supporting Convergence phenomena reveals sophisticated healing applications. Through careful use of what they term "Harmonic Integration Codes," Andromedian teams can facilitate smooth timeline mergers using specific sound patterns.

These acoustic technologies demonstrate remarkable effectiveness in supporting consciousness expansion during transition phases. Advanced monitoring systems employed by Andromedian researchers show interesting patterns in what they call "Timeline Merger Sequences" - predictable stages that occur during major Convergence events. This understanding helps guide the timing and application of various support measures during critical integration phases.

The Convergence process also activates what Andromedians term "Dormant DNA Potentials" - aspects of human genetic coding that become accessible through exposure to merged timeline frequencies. This remarkable phenomenon facilitates unprecedented opportunities for biological and consciousness evolution.

Of particular importance are the "Unity Grid Nodes" - specialized points in Earth's energy field that serve as natural amplifiers for Convergence frequencies.

These powerful locations help maintain coherence during periods of intense timeline integration, ensuring smooth transition through various evolutionary thresholds.

The relationship between Earth's elemental kingdoms and Convergence dynamics reveals fascinating patterns. Through what Andromedians call "Elemental Consciousness Integration," the natural world begins to demonstrate enhanced abilities to process and transmit unified timeline frequencies. This remarkable phenomenon helps stabilize the physical environment during major transition phases.

Advanced healing protocols developed for Convergence support operate at quantum levels of reality creation. These "Unified Field Technologies" can address potential integration challenges across multiple timeline streams simultaneously, ensuring optimal outcomes during merger phases.

The Convergence process also initiates what Andromedian scientists term "Consciousness Field Expansion" - a natural phenomenon where human awareness begins to spontaneously access multiple timeline possibilities simultaneously.

This remarkable expansion of perception creates unprecedented opportunities for personal and collective transformation. The role of crystal technologies in supporting Convergence phenomena continues to evolve. Advanced crystalline matrices utilized by Andromedian teams demonstrate extraordinary capabilities for processing vast amounts of timeline data while maintaining perfect energetic balance.

These sophisticated tools prove invaluable in monitoring and supporting smooth integration processes. Looking ahead, Andromedian researchers anticipate what they call "The Great Unity" - a state of consciousness where humanity naturally perceives and operates within unified timeline fields. This remarkable achievement represents the fulfillment of ancient prophecies about Earth's cosmic awakening and transformation.

The future implications of successful Convergence extend far beyond Earth's immediate reality sphere. As a living demonstration of harmonious timeline integration, Earth's journey serves as a crucial template for similar evolutionary processes throughout the galaxy. This represents one of the most significant aspects of Earth's cosmic purpose and potential.

The depth of consciousness integration during Convergence phases reveals what Andromedians term "Unity State Realization" - a profound level of awareness where individual consciousness naturally resonates with unified field potentials. This extraordinary state of being represents the fulfillment of humanity's innate potential for cosmic consciousness.

Advanced timeline analysis reveals interesting patterns in what Andromedian researchers call "Final Integration Sequences" - the delicate processes through which various reality streams achieve ultimate harmony. These sophisticated observations provide crucial insights into how consciousness evolution completes its grand cosmic cycle.

The final stages of Convergence initiate what Andromedians term "Cosmic Memory Restoration" - a remarkable phenomenon where Earth consciousness naturally accesses its full multidimensional heritage. This profound awakening creates unprecedented opportunities for healing and transformation across all levels of planetary existence.

"As Earth and Andromeda dance across space and time, their sacred alignment opens doorways for humanity's quantum evolution."

Epilogue

A Message from the Andromedian Timeline Masters

As we conclude this exploration of Earth's timeline journey, we offer these final reflections from our perspective as witnesses and supporters of your remarkable evolutionary process. The story we have shared is not merely an account of external intervention or technological achievement. It is, at its heart, a love letter to Earth's extraordinary potential and the remarkable courage demonstrated by all who choose to participate in this grand evolutionary experiment.

We observe with profound appreciation how human consciousness continues to expand beyond limited perceptions of reality. Your growing ability to sense and interact with multiple timeline possibilities represents one of the most remarkable achievements in your sector of the galaxy. The journey ahead holds extraordinary promise.

As timeline convergence accelerates, you will discover capabilities within yourselves that transcend current understanding of human potential. The activation of dormant DNA codes, the expansion of perceptual abilities, and the natural emergence of unified consciousness awareness represent just the beginning of your cosmic awakening.

Remember that our role has always been one of support rather than direction. The choices that shape Earth's future emerge from the collective wisdom of your own planetary consciousness. We simply provide energetic assistance and occasional guidance when requested.

Your planet stands at the threshold of what we term "Universal Integration" - a state of consciousness where artificial barriers between different levels of reality naturally dissolve.

This remarkable transition represents not an ending, but a profound new beginning in Earth's cosmic journey. The skills and understanding you develop through this process will serve not only Earth's evolution but will provide invaluable wisdom for other worlds approaching similar transformational thresholds.

Your journey becomes a living library of experience, offering crucial insights into harmonious planetary ascension processes. As we conclude this transmission, we remind you that the timeline mastery we have described is not external to your own consciousness.

These capabilities represent natural aspects of your multidimensional heritage, awakening now in perfect alignment with cosmic evolutionary cycles.

The future holds possibilities that transcend current human imagination. Trust in your inner wisdom, honor your natural connection to Earth's living systems, and remember that you are never alone in this remarkable journey of consciousness expansion and timeline integration.

With deepest appreciation for your courage and commitment to evolutionary excellence,

- **The Andromedian Timeline Masters**

As the veils between dimensions grow thinner, the wisdom keepers of Andromeda extend their light as a bridge between worlds."

Made in the USA
Columbia, SC
14 February 2025